KIRSTIE ROWSON

The Merry Players

First published by If In Doubt Create 2020

This novel is entirely a work of fiction. The names, characters and incidents portrayed in it are the work of the author's imagination. Any resemblance to actual persons, living or dead, events or localities is entirely coincidental.

Kirstie Rowson asserts the moral right to be identified as the author of this work.

Cover illustration and title lettering by Kirstie Rowson. Cover layout and design by Sarah Goodwin. Cover font Victopian by Hannah Marks.

With thanks to Antonia Prescott for her fantastic editing advice. And with thanks to my brilliant proofreaders for their eagle-eyes and honest and kind feedback.

First edition

ISBN: 978-1-8380505-7-3

This book was professionally typeset on Reedsy. Find out more at reedsy.com

For my brilliant nieces and nephew
who are all so present in these pages.
Love love love
Auntie K x

CHAPTER ONE

Jackson knelt in the wings of The Merry Theatre, peering through the gap in the drapes onto the floodlit stage as he did night after night. Having delivered his lines, Harry was striding towards him at a pace. Jackson tried to shuffle to one side on his knees but wasn't quite quick enough and Harry's foot stopped abruptly as it hit Jackson's leg.

"Who's that?" Harry whispered in shock, glancing down in the darkness. A look of friendly recognition appeared on his face, "Any closer and you'll be *on* the stage!"

Jackson smiled and muttered an apology but Harry had already sped away around the back of the set heading for the dressing rooms. Jackson edged back towards the sliver of light. The stage was ablaze with activity as the two lead actors, Seamus and Emma, darted from one side to the other. The audience watched them, hypnotised. A wave of laughter filled the auditorium as Emma flounced off stage towards Jackson's hiding place. This time he was able to shuffle to one side to avoid a collision. She was smiling to herself as she entered the wing and as her eyes adjusted to the black she spotted Jackson.

"Aren't you bored of this play by now?" she laughed quietly. Jackson tipped his head to one side as Emma instinctively reached to ruffle his hair. She'd done this since he could

1

remember and he was getting a bit sick of being treated like a child. Emma smiled faintly and then spun round to keep an eye on the action ready for her next cue. Jackson watched as she mouthed the lines silently to herself. How could she remember so many words? And how was she brave enough to step onto the stage in front of all those people with all those eyes on her. His eyes followed her as she stepped back into the play, into the bright spotlights and he knew that he would never have the courage to do it again.

In the half-light Jackson could just about see the people in the front couple of rows looking up like children. Some with wide eyes, some with gaping mouths, some settled back in their chairs utterly absorbed. Jackson recognised several regulars amongst the faces. There was Mr Fothergill constantly readjusting his cravat. His wife, sharp-cheeked and stern, forever tapping his hand to stop him doing it. There were sisters Marjorie and Phyllis, dressed up to the nines and in the same seats they always had. And he could just about spot his friend Oliver from school with his parents either side of him, bobbing around trying to see over the shoulders of the person in front of him.

As Jackson continued to look along the second row, his eyes settled on a weaselly-looking man who was sitting by the aisle with his arms folded in a defensive way that made Jackson curious. The man was wearing a perfectly-fitting dark grey suit with a thin silvery tie that looked like a silver fish shimmering on his shirt. His hair was a bit too long and slicked back with wax that should have made it look glossy but only succeeded in making it look like it needed a good wash. He had a fixed expression of mild disgust on his face, his pointy nose pointing pointily. Jackson noticed that his eyes weren't watching the actors as they moved around the stage, rather, they were studying the surrounding details, the fraying curtains, the scuffed floorboards, the slightly faded scenery. As if he was making a mental checklist of The Merry Theatre's faults.

The audience suddenly erupted with surprise and delight. Harry had performed an elaborate fake fall, which had prompted a big laugh as always. Jackson realised that even while the other actors on the stage found it hard to conceal their amusement, the weaselly man's face remained cemented in a sneer. Then, even more strangely, all of a sudden he lowered his head as if wanting to hide his face from view. He proceeded to pull out a small notebook and pencil from his inside pocket. Flipping the notebook open neatly, he scribbled some words quickly as Jackson watched, feeling increasingly irritated. What was the man writing? More importantly, *why* was he writing? In the middle of a show. In the dark. As quickly as he had started writing, he stopped, snapped the notebook shut and put it back in his pocket. He then took out another item. Jackson watched as he turned his hand towards the stage. He seemed to be holding a small hand mirror which made his palm shimmer in the darkness.

Jackson stared as the man turned his hand this way and that, pretending to straighten his cuffs, the light glimmering in his palm. Harry, who was about to deliver his funniest line of the play, stopped for the briefest moment, losing his pace and stammering over his words. The audience started to laugh and then stopped, confused. Harry exited from the scene, screeching to a halt and breathing in deeply. Catching sight of Jackson shifting on his knees on the floor, he put his hand to his chest and exclaimed in a whisper,

"Goodness, Jackson! Forgot you were there! Got a bit dazzled by one of the lights for a moment. I'll have to have a word with George to get that fixed."

"That man in the audience did it …" Jackson started to say but just as quickly as he had run from the stage Harry stepped back on, picking up his cue perfectly.

Jackson turned his attention back to the second row and to his surprise there was an empty flipped-up seat where the weaselly man had been. He scanned the auditorium quickly but it was too dark at the back to see which way he might have gone. Without a thought, he turned and slipped away, passed George, the old Lighting Director, who was frantically checking his panel of switches and wondering what had just happened to distract Harry. Jackson continued down to the side door, which led out to the side of the stalls. He knew if his parents spotted him, he would be in trouble for disturbing the show so he sidled along in the shadows barely breathing. As he reached the back of the stalls, suddenly, CRUNCH! Something squished under Jackson's foot and several faces looked across at him in the half-light with a variety of startled expressions as they were snapped out of their reverie by the unexpected sound. Jackson froze and looked down to see an ice cream tub crumpled under his foot. The melting mess that had been inside was soaking into the carpet.

"I'm sorry!" he mouthed to the owner of the ice cream who glared back at him. He could feel his cheeks flushing red and was grateful for the darkness as he hurried away towards the back doors of the auditorium. He opened the door, just a few inches and squeezed through the gap into the lobby, letting the door close quietly. A ripple of muffled laughter could be heard from the audience behind him.

The lobby was empty but Jackson felt a chill in the air from where the front doors of the building had just swung shut. He pushed the door just in time to see the weaselly man disappear over the road. The old town hall opposite the Merry Theatre had been covered in scaffolding and hidden by tarpaulin for months and the whole town was intrigued about what was secretly going on inside. Jackson had often looked at it on his way to school and wondered. There had been speculation that a rich businessman had bought it to be his new home and lavish deliveries of plush carpets and golden chandeliers seemed to arrive on an almost daily basis. Tonight the canvas covering the building rustled loudly in the breeze. The man seemed to know exactly where he was going and slipped between a gap in the cover, glancing back over his shoulder as he did so. Jackson quickly tucked himself behind a post box, just in time. He didn't think the man had seen him but he still felt a shiver down his spine.

He bent down to inspect his foot to see how much ice cream was on his shoe. Only then realising that there was a presence behind him. He turned slowly, fully expecting his Dad to be staring at him disapprovingly and was relieved to find it was just Stanley, one of the oldest ushers, who was polishing the glass cabinets that housed the show posters. Stanley was as deaf as a post and whistling to himself out of tune. He seemed not to have noticed anything at all. As he turned towards the front doors, having finished his task, he spotted Jackson and clutched his hand to his chest.

"You gave me a start!" he exclaimed and then looked at Jackson curiously as he continued to study his shoe.

"Ice cream," Jackson stated loudly, as if that explained everything. "Did you see a man in a dark grey suit?"

"Um…" Stanley mumbled, "I don't think so…"

They made their way inside and Stanley stepped behind the ticket desk, leaning down to put the cloth back in one of the drawers.

"I'm sure I closed that…" Stanley muttered and Jackson clocked his quizzical expression as he stared into the cash drawer and then shook his head, like he was reassuring himself.

"Everything ok, Stanley?"

The old man replied, "Yes, yes."

Jackson felt uneasy. Applause suddenly erupted from inside the auditorium. It was the end of the show and Jackson, realising he was already at risk of being scolded for not being where he was meant to be, backstage, turned to head back out of the front doors. He was less likely to get caught if he sneaked round the side of the theatre.

"Don't tell Dad you saw me," Jackson smiled cheekily and disappeared, leaving Stanley still looking in confusion at the cash drawer.

CHAPTER TWO

The next morning, Jackson noticed his Dad, Albert kneeling next to the stain on the carpet in the stalls. He was looking irritated as he inspected the damage.

"Can't the audience just be a bit more careful? Look at the state of it! It's not like we can afford to just replace the carpet! There's plenty more we need to spend our money on before that."

Knowing he was more than a little to blame but not fancying confessing this to his Dad, Jackson offered to get a bucket of soapy water to clean the stain. Albert accepted his son's offer and stormed off, cursing to himself. Once Jackson had done his best to clean the carpet, he made his way up to the stage with a mop and bucket in hand, slopping soapy water over the wooden boards. He looked up across the empty seats and found himself remembering how it had felt to be a part of the performance. His fellow actors projecting their voices to the crowd, the lights so bright he could barely see the audience but he had felt their warmth and energy. And then he remembered the tightening in his throat as he realised he had forgotten everything, his head pounding, the sound becoming more muffled, a distorted laugh, his heart in his mouth.

It had been the final show of the Christmas season. He only had a small part to play but it was the first time his Dad had given him a role. Jackson had felt like he was doing it for him, like he was following in his Dad's footsteps. Striding out on to the stage, delivering his lines and feeling the crowd's warmth as they applauded at the end of each night had been amazing. Then the last night had arrived. It was only a small mistake. He had only missed one line. But it had left Emma looking at him blankly under the spotlight, hesitating and willing him to find his words. He remembered the look on her face and the prickle of heat that had crept from his neck to his cheeks. He remembered how he had stuttered and the one solitary laugh from the stalls, breaking the silence. Then another giggle had followed and another and then Emma smiled. A smile that he had taken to mean that she was amused by his mistake, that he wasn't good enough. He didn't deserve to be adored like his Dad, the beloved Albert Merry. A smile that she, of course, had only ever meant to be supportive.

Suddenly his Dad was beside him, watching him gaze out across the theatre and Jackson was immediately back in the present moment.

"So, when are we going to get you back on this stage?" Albert asked.

Jackson winced, instantly feeling his Dad's disappointment in him. Before he could answer, they were interrupted by his Mum, Martha appearing from the wings. His Dad smiled at her fondly, forgetting their conversation.

"There's a visitor for us. It's Mr Greengold," his Mum said gesturing at the man's presence with her hand.

Mr Greengold stepped tentatively from the shadows, removing a black trilby hat from his head. He was carrying a briefcase in his left hand and fumbled with the hat a little as he greeted Albert with what Jackson imagined to be a cold, clammy palm.

"Ah, Mr Greengold, fabulous, yes, great, ok, so yes. Follow me," his Dad tripped over his words as he greeted the man. Jackson couldn't help but notice that his Dad seemed a little nervous. His Mum was smiling through slightly gritted teeth, which was unlike her usual sunny disposition.

"I'll join you in a moment," she said, staring steadily at her husband.

Albert led the way from the stage towards his office with Mr Greengold shuffling behind him, his head lowered in a rather sombre way. Jackson watched the briefcase held tightly in the man's hand and wondered what was inside.

"Nothing for you to worry about," his Mum said, seeing her son's expression as the two men disappeared into the wings. "Why don't you start to get the costumes ready for tonight while we're in our meeting?"

"I'll put this away first," Jackson said, pointing to the mop and bucket. He watched his Mum leave the stage, knowing he had another plan in mind. He was still curious about the weaselly man from the night before. And he was still intrigued about the building opposite and what was going on inside. But now he had something else to think about too. Who was Mr Greengold? And why was his Dad so nervous around him? And why did his Mum suddenly seem so tense? When he'd woken up this morning he had planned to sneak out of the theatre and across the road to see what was behind the scaffolding. But now there were more immediate things to attend to. He waited a couple of minutes until he was certain that his parents were behind closed doors, then he gently placed the mop on the floor and tiptoed as quietly as he could towards their office.

The office was at the end of the corridor, past the door to the prop store and up a small flight of stairs that were so old they creaked even if you glanced at them. Jackson stood at the bottom of the stairs and listened as hard as he could. The only sound was a muffled exchange of words. The tone was serious, or as serious as muffles could be. He looked around, considering what to do next. He really needed to hear their conversation. The bannister was painted white but the paint was flaking. He picked at a flake as he stood straining his ears and absent-mindedly placed his right foot on the bottom step. 'CREEEEAK!' went the step. Jackson gasped and pulled his foot away as if he had stepped on hot coals. The muffles fell silent and the floorboards in the office squeaked. He heard his Dad clear his throat. He sprang backwards and dived into the prop store, closing the door behind him as quickly and quietly as possible.

"So I'll make an assessment and let you know the theatre's worth," a voice suddenly said in the darkness. Jackson was taken aback and looked around him. Looking up, he realised, there was a vent in the wall, high up on the right-hand side that led straight into the office. It was Mr Greengold's voice!

"But I'm not going to sell," Jackson heard his Dad say. Sell? He felt his heart stop.

"Yes, we're not at that stage yet, are we?" Martha asked.

Mr Greengold continued, "You may have no choice if the sums don't add up."

There was silence from the office for a moment and then Albert spoke, "It won't come to that."

"But this will be your last production for some time if you don't find investment. You simply don't have the funds to put on another show."

"I just don't understand it," Martha sighed. "We have a good crowd every night. We've always been fine in the past. I can't make sense of where the money's going. Can we afford to get to the end of this run at least?"

"Just paying wages to the actors already puts you in the red."

His parents sounded more serious than Jackson had ever heard them before, "I see," they said in unison.

"Well, thank you for your time, Mr and Mrs Merry. I've still got to assess how much everything in the theatre is worth so I'll be in touch when I've finished my report and we can fix a time to make a list so that we can give an exact figure to potential buyers. I already know of one possible interested party."

Martha and Albert remained silent. Jackson heard chairs scrape on the floor and the click of the clasps on Mr Greengold's briefcase. The office door opened and he heard heavy footsteps and the high-pitched *CREAK* of the stairs as the group headed towards the stage door where Jackson hoped his parents would tell Mr Greengold to go and never come back. How could he even suggest that the theatre was for sale? Jackson knew he hadn't liked this seemingly mild-mannered man from the moment he had laid eyes on him.

He slumped down on a pile of dust sheets. He needed to think. As well as props for the current show, the room was full of boxes, chairs and bits and bobs that had been used in various shows over the years. His parents never threw anything away, in case they needed the same props and set pieces again. They were careful with their money and thought ahead, which is

11

why he didn't understand how they could possibly be in such financial strife. Was the Merry Theatre really in that much trouble?

Suddenly Jackson heard footsteps. They were tip-toey and clicky. They were coming his way. He picked himself up from his slouched position on the pile of sheets and as the footsteps got louder and came to a stop outside the door, he lurched towards the light switch and flooded the room with light from the bare lightbulb that hung from the middle of the ceiling. The door handle turned with a clunk and the door flew open. His Mum gasped.

"Goodness, Jackson! What are you doing hiding in here? You gave me such a fright!" she garbled, clearly flustered.

Jackson thought quickly, "I didn't want to disturb your meeting."

"Right." His Mum accepted his answer but still didn't have a clue why her son was in the props store.

Jackson spoke quickly to distract her, "I thought I'd bring some of the props to you in the wardrobe room. For tonight."

"You are a good boy," she smiled as she stepped into the room. She looked around the shelves and floor at the hodgepodge of boxes, piles of dust sheets and jumble. "We really need to have a tidy up in here!"

"Mum…" Jackson began. "Is the theatre in trouble?" He looked at her intently, watching as she reached for a box of crockery.

She avoided looking at him, "Why would you think that?"

"I just wondered. You and Dad seem worried."

His Mum stopped for a moment, clutching the box in her arms and turned to her son. "It's nothing for you to worry about. Try not to bother your Dad with questions. He's got a plan. You know him, he always has a plan." With that, she smiled a tight smile and left the room, calling behind her, "Will you bring that box of hats out for me?"

Jackson grabbed the box and followed his Mum into the corridor. All he could think about was how much he needed to find an excuse to rummage around in the office to see if he could find any clues about how bad things really were. He also wanted to get out of the theatre to satisfy his curiosity about the old town hall. He remembered he had some money left in his money box and asked if he could go to the paper shop to buy a comic. He was pretty pleased with his cunning excuse. His Mum even gave him an extra few coins and told him to get some sweets too as a treat for helping out. And although he felt bad for lying to her, this was not just important, it was IMPORTANT in capital letters.

CHAPTER THREE

Outside it was cold and breezy and the street was unusually quiet. Jackson quickly crossed the road and headed towards the scaffolding. It criss-crossed right up to the roof and had sheets of tarpaulin stretching from top to bottom obscuring the view. The old town hall had been in a state of disrepair for almost three years. Jackson hadn't paid any attention to it before but had heard his parents talk about the Lady Mayoress, a frivolous lady named Victoria Strudwick, who had thought the old town hall *most unsuitable* and had ploughed a large amount of her own family's money into a brand *new* town hall which included a fancy penthouse apartment for herself. With no one looking after it, the old building had become something of an eyesore and so, when the scaffolding had first been constructed it had caused a huge stir around the town. The rumour was that it had been bought by a rich businessman but no one seemed to know why. Maybe if Jackson had paid attention, he thought, he would have an idea of who the weaselly man was and why he could get into the building. Was he the new owner? And why had he been trying to disrupt their show and then run off into the night?

Jackson stood in the spot where the Weasel, as he had now

named him, had disappeared. There was a small gap in the tarpaulin where he had ducked under the scaffolding bars. Jackson looked around as casually as he could. Luckily there was no one around to see as he edged behind the flapping material. His heart was beating in his chest like a bird trying to escape a cage. The light was gloomy but he could see the windows and doors along the front of the building. The window ledges were made of white stone that was weathered and dirty. They were level with Jackson's shoulders so he knew he would be able to peer over them and to see what was inside if he could just get close enough. There were tall, ornate double doors halfway along the front wall that looked very heavy and like they had been sanded down ready to be painted. Above the doors, Jackson could see the outline of a rectangular sign that had been hung on brass fixings but a sheet was covering it so it was impossible to read it.

Jackson had read about spies in stories and thought it would be best if he had his back against the wall, edging along as if he was on a stakeout. As his back scraped along the wall, he realised he had been holding his breath for as long as he had been behind the tarpaulin so took a big, desperate gulp of air. Then breathed out slowly, trying to calm himself down. He reached the first window and very slowly turned his head to try to peer inside. He was disappointed to find that a thick pair of curtains were covering the window so he couldn't see in. He would have to go along to the next one. He reached it easily and tried to peer inside. Once again his view was blocked by heavy drapes. He would have to go past the big double doors to the windows on the other side.

Jackson steeled himself and looked along the wall past the doors. There was a stone step at the base of them that he needed to scamper round before he could be against the wall again. He stared at the door, listening for signs of life. Nothing. He decided to count to three and then run for it. One. He could hear himself puffing anxiously. Two. Another lungful. Three. And he pushed off from his back foot and ran. It was only a few steps but it felt like everything was happening in slow motion.

He reached the wall and pinned himself against it, banging his head as he did so.

"Ouch!" he exclaimed and then told himself to "Shush!" And then told himself to shush *silently* in his head for saying shush out loud. He edged towards the next window. The curtains in this window were closed but there was a slight gap between them where they weren't fully drawn. Brilliant! Jackson manoeuvred himself, ducking down under the stone windowsill ready to bob up and see through the window.

He slowly moved up, terrified that the Weasel would be glaring back at him from the other side. He breathed a sigh of relief as all he could see was a room. Well, not so much a room as a lobby and a rather grand lobby at that, with high ceilings and a gargantuan and garish gold-framed portrait of a rather portly and dismal-looking gentleman with grey greasy hair on the wall, facing him. It looked like somebody had laid grey string on the man's head. On each side of the portrait there was a set of black double doors, with whirls and swirls of gold painted on them and great big brass door handles that clashed with the gold. Jackson couldn't see very much but he could see the carpet was inky blue and deep and plush. It looked like it would swallow you up if you stepped on it. If he really strained to look, Jackson could just see the start of an ostentatious, sweeping staircase. Everything was very, very over the top, very, very new and very, very flashy. Perhaps it was the grey, portly, gloomy gentleman's house? Why else would there be a portrait of him on the wall?

As Jackson continued to study and puzzle over the gold design on one of the black doors, he suddenly realised that the door appeared to be opening. And as he looked more closely, he realised that it was *actually* opening and as it opened he realised that the person opening it was none other than the Weasel. Thankfully the Weasel's weaselly eyes were looking the other way as he was deep in conversation with somebody. He looked just as pointy as Jackson remembered as he sidled into the grand hall. He wondered who he was in conversation with. And then he saw. A man who looked like he had been squeezed and squished into his suit. A man with grey stringy hair on his head. The man from the portrait! He was barking orders, like a highly-strung Sergeant Major. Jackson was wide-eyed as he realised that the two men were heading towards the front doors. In fact, they were just about to walk through them.

Quick as a flash, he turned and looked around frantically for his escape route. He would have to go back under the tarpaulin. He spied a small gap in the corner and scrambled towards it, throwing himself onto the ground. Quick! He lifted it as much as he could and pulled himself along with his elbows, digging his toes into the pavement and pushing himself forward as fast as he could. Shuffling and scrabbling to escape. He heard the heavy clunk and click of the front doors as the Weasel and string-haired man got closer. He was almost under. The heel of his shoe caught on the tarpaulin briefly and he tensed up his toes to keep it on his foot. As the doors swung open and the two men emerged, Jackson was through and clambering to his feet. He could hear the men's voices on the other side of the tarpaulin and stood frozen to the spot, afraid to move in case they heard him.

The Weasel and the string-haired man stood at the entrance to the building, looking back at the doors. The facade loomed high above them. The larger of the two men was growling.

"We are opening NEXT WEEK," he hissed through his teeth. "Make. This. Right." His voice sharp with anger. "Where. Are. The. Lights? Can you tell me that?" If Jackson had had x-ray vision he would have seen the man's hair slip down across his eyes and the awkward flip of his head to put it back in place. "How can we open without LIGHTS?"

The Weasel clamped his teeth together in irritation. "I've already told you, my *dear* brother. They will be in place in time. We agreed I would look after it." He paused and puffed air out through his nostrils, "And I will."

The string-haired man growled and his shoe squeaked as he turned to go back inside. The Weasel followed him and as the doors slammed shut, Jackson could only just make out what he said, "Albert won't know what's hit him."

Did he hear correctly? Did he say Albert? How did they know his Dad? His mind racing, he turned and ran, as fast as he could, back home.

CHAPTER FOUR

As the evening show approached, Jackson was in his usual spot helping to prepare the stage for the actors. He positioned the chairs just so for the opening scene. He then placed a glass of water on the table for the moment in the play where Emma threw it over Harry and made sure the pile of books that Seamus used as a prop was ready for him to grab as he strode on to the stage from the wing. All of his friends were on school holidays and had disappeared on trips across the country to see relatives. Even Oliver had gone to his grandma's to spend two weeks by the sea. Jackson didn't remember ever going away on holiday. His parents were always working, which meant he had to make his own entertainment. And so most evenings, while they worked, Jackson worked too, helping out with the theatre preparations and watching the plays night after night. His Mum was at the stage door signing in the actors as they arrived. Jackson wandered towards the office to look for his Dad. The door was closed but this time he creaked up the stairs and knocked. He could hear his Dad's voice inside.

"Yes, ten o'clock tomorrow will be fine, thank you Mr Greengold. See you then." There was a click as the telephone receiver was replaced. And then, "Come in?"

Jackson pushed the door and poked his head round the side.

Albert was attempting to tidy his desk and to put papers in a pile. His son noticed that many of the pages were covered in scribbled sums and crosses.

"Always so much filing to do!" his Dad said trying to sound light-hearted.

"Dad, are you selling the theatre?" Jackson asked directly. He watched as his Dad avoided making eye contact.

"Of course not! Whatever gave you that idea?"

Jackson gazed at him. He could see that his usually sparkly eyes were full of concern. "Are we in trouble?" he asked.

"Now, why would we be in trouble? Everything's ok." Albert could see that his son wasn't convinced. "I promised your great-grandfather I would always look after this place," he added, somewhat wistfully as he rose from his chair, walking towards the door.

"But what did that man want yesterday? And you said you couldn't afford new carpet?"

His Dad stopped and turned abruptly, "Jackson, it's grown up business."

Jackson couldn't help himself. "I'm not a child, Dad. There's something going on. There was a man in the audience trying to distract Harry. He went into the building across the road. Do you know the man who owns it? I heard them talking and…"

His Dad looked at him, he could see the tension in his face. "I haven't got time for this, Jackson. Not now. I need to make sure everything is ready for the show." And with that he swept past his son and headed for the door.

As they made their way down the corridor, towards the dressing rooms, Jackson could hear the familiar hubbub of the actors warming up their voices ready for their performance.

Emma was striding towards them reciting her lines under her breath. She acknowledged both father and son with smiling eyes while continuing her recital. The charismatic lead actor, Seamus O'Callahan was further along, straightening his jacket, stretching his arms out and bending his knees as if limbering up for some exercise. Harry was singing scales as if readying himself for an opera. He did the same thing every night, note-perfect, although there were definitely no songs in the play. As Albert whisked by, with Jackson following closely behind, Harry called after him and started to walk quickly alongside him.

"Albert, I was... Er... I was wondering if we could maybe have a chat again about perhaps adding a musical number?" Harry paused momentarily as Albert stopped in his tracks and spun on his heel to look at him. "To the opening of the show?" Harry continued. "Or the closing of the show? Or even just for the closing night. I know I've asked before but I was just thinking..."

"Harry," Albert looked him in the eyes and put his hand on his shoulder kindly. "I'm sorry, I don't *want* to say no again. Your voice is magnificent. There's just no call for any songs in the play."

Jackson thought Harry, who usually always had a flicker of light in his eyes, looked rather defeated.

"Let's think about what we can do in the next show, yes?" With that, Albert moved on leaving Harry looking resigned.

Albert acknowledged everyone as he walked, patting them on the back, wishing them luck, telling them to 'break a leg' and weaving his way towards the stalls to check everything was in place before the doors were opened for the evening's audience.

Jackson continued following him.

"There's something going on, Dad. I *need* to talk to you…"

Albert stopped, spinning round to look Jackson in the eye. "Not now. I have too much on my plate to worry about some man in the audience. We're not in one of your *stories*!" Jackson flinched but his Dad didn't miss a beat. "I promised your great-grandfather that I would keep this place going no matter what and that is what I am *trying* to do. When you're older, you'll understand that sometimes there are bigger problems to think about."

With that he turned and carried on walking. Jackson followed, silenced by his Dad's blunt words. He may be ten but he wasn't a child, why did everyone insist on treating him like he was. Well, he would show them. He would find out what was going on and fix it!

They passed George, the Lighting Director, who was busy testing a multitude of switches on his board with his half-moon glasses perched at the end of his nose. Jackson had watched George enough times to know every single change of lighting in the play. He was absolutely certain that the flash of light that had distracted Harry wasn't George's fault. As they passed by, he looked up and nodded at Albert to confirm all was in order and Jackson and his Dad continued through the side-door into the stalls. Jackson loved it when the place was empty. He was one of the only people who ever had the theatre to himself. He looked around the cavernous space as they walked along. With the house lights on he could see the elaborate, swirling carvings on the ceiling, now slightly dull in colour but still just as ornate as they had been in his great-grandfather's day. A chandelier hung in the centre, it maintained its grandeur but his Dad had mentioned several times that he couldn't afford to have it cleaned. There was no dress circle or grand circle like Jackson had seen in pictures of other theatres but that was part of the Merry's charm. The floor had a slight slope to it so that every seat had a good view and everyone felt close to the action on the stage. Jackson looked along the rows of seats and then down at his Dad's worn shoes as they landed purposefully on the worn carpet. He thought about the sumptuous carpet across the road and imagined his feet sinking into it as he walked.

All of a sudden, the right-hand door at the back of the stalls swung open and his Mum rushed into the auditorium. There was a quick burst of chatter from the audience waiting outside as the door opened and silence fell again as it closed.

"Albert!" Martha exclaimed as she rushed towards them.

"What's happened? Are you alright?" Albert asked.

Martha's eyebrows were knitted together in a frown, her voice was high-pitched, "Someone's vandalised the posters outside! Look!"

Only then did Jackson notice that his Mum was holding a wide strip of white paper in her hands. "These are stuck across every one! Stanley's taking them down now."

Albert took the paper from his wife and studied the black writing on it. It read, 'CLOSING DOWN'. His Dad's face went pale.

"Who would do such a thing? Our customers are asking Stanley and the other ushers what's going on," Martha continued.

"Are we closing down?" was the only thing Jackson could think to say.

"Of course not," his Mum snapped. Jackson felt himself recoil and his Mum looked at him apologetically, "I'm sorry, I'm just…" she said quickly and trailed off as Albert walked out into the foyer and the chatter from the audience got louder. He was immediately accosted by a sophisticated gentleman in a dinner jacket with the shiniest shoes Jackson had ever seen.

"Albert, my dear fellow. It's not true is it? Closing down?" he bellowed, enough that anyone who had not already seen the signs outside would hear.

"No, of course not!" Albert smiled. "Seems to be somebody's idea of a joke." He tried to laugh light-heartedly but his voice sounded weak. Jackson's Mum was already busy talking to another man in a blue velvet jacket.

"No, not at all… No… We're not sure where they came from," Jackson heard her say.

While questions were fired at his parents, he weaved his way between ladies in posh frocks and men in their Sunday best. He was short enough not to draw too much attention to himself. Towards the front doors he felt the freshness of the evening air on his face as he stepped out into the light of the entrance. Stanley was busily scraping at one of the 'closing down' signs with a blade, doing his best to remove it from the glass cabinet that housed one of the show posters. Jackson looked along the outside of the theatre. There were four posters and two of them still had the banners on.

Back inside the foyer, his parents continued to be inundated with questions. "Why are you closing?" "When are you closing?" "You kept that quiet!" Jackson watched as his Dad tried his best to command the crowd, standing on tiptoes and raising his voice to be heard.

"Ok!" Albert waved his arms, getting a little exasperated. "Ok!" he repeated. A hush fell over the audience.

"I don't know who thought we were closing down. Please don't believe what you see on our posters tonight. We are not closing our doors. In fact, we are opening them for you in about five minutes!" His Dad's attempt to lighten the mood was met with a ripple of laughter and in his best showman's voice, he added, "On with the show!" Jackson watched as his Dad held his arms out by way of welcome and beamed at his patrons, hiding his obvious confusion.

CHAPTER FIVE

The next morning, Jackson jumped out of bed, his head buzzing with questions. Did Mr Greengold put the closing signs up? He was the one, after all, who had mentioned selling the theatre. Was the theatre closing down? He had to find out more about the men across the road. Did this Mr Greengold *know* the Weasel and the string-haired man? And why had they mentioned his Dad? Jackson took a deep breath. First things first, he had to be in the prop store at ten o'clock to hear about these sums that Mr Greengold was doing. Jackson really wasn't keen on maths. He couldn't understand why an adult would actually *choose* to do it as a job but he wanted to know a whole lot more about why Mr Greengold was encouraging his Dad to sell.

Jackson changed out of his pyjamas and pulled on trousers and a jumper before opening the curtains. It had been raining overnight and it was still coming down in buckets. He clomped down the stairs, deep in thought. If the theatre was going to be sold, would their home be sold too? The new owners wouldn't want the old ones living on their doorstep. The house was part of the theatre. Jackson had been born here, he didn't know any different. Their home may have been small but it fitted the Merry family perfectly with two bedrooms, a neat little kitchen and a cosy sitting room. One wall of Jackson's bedroom was covered in posters from previous shows and his parents had built him some shelves that were home to his treasured collection of stories. Picture books that he couldn't bear to be parted from and novels that he adored. Comics that he collected and non-fiction books full of wonderful facts. He loved them all. His Mum had painted the ceiling dark blue and stuck on white paper stars that seemed to glow in the moonlight. There was a rug covering the floorboards where Jackson often sat and read with his back leaning against the bed. His Dad had told him that the rug had once belonged to his great-grandfather, Billy and it had been in the house when they had inherited it. His sash window was framed with red curtains, made from the same material as the stage curtains and his view was of the cobbled courtyard and the stage door where the actors came and went.

Downstairs the sitting room had a fireplace and a worn sofa and armchair that had also been inherited from Billy. As they were always in the theatre, this room was hardly used but Jackson's Mum had covered the sofa with a patterned bedspread that his great-grandmother, Constance, had handed down. It was colourful and vibrant, just like Constance had been. There was a collection of old family photos on the mantelpiece. Next to the sitting room was the kitchen, with its wooden worktops and well-loved table and chairs where Jackson's Mum often taught him to make cakes and where they all cooked roast dinners together on Sundays. Most mornings when Jackson came down for breakfast he would find one of his parents poring over paperwork at the table. Scripts and contracts and now he came to think of it, accounts and sums that they would often gather up and tidy away in a drawer when he emerged. He had always assumed they were just clearing the way for breakfast but, now he came to think of it, perhaps they were squirrelling things away that they didn't want him to see.

In fact, his Mum was at the kitchen table now and sure enough, there were papers spread across the surface. His Dad was standing at the worktop spreading some butter onto a thick piece of toast. He stopped talking mid-sentence when he saw Jackson in the doorway. His Mum sprang up and shoved the papers into the drawer by the sink.

"Morning!" his parents chorused unnaturally. "Toast?"

Jackson accepted the offer and looked at them suspiciously as he sat down on one of the rickety chairs. His Dad passed a piece of hot, buttery toast to him with a smile.

"What are you going to do today?" his Mum asked. "Maybe invite one of your school friends round. Don't want you getting bored in the holidays."

"Think I'll just do some reading," Jackson replied, thinking there was absolutely no chance of him getting bored with the investigations he had to do. He had decided to stop asking his parents questions, it wasn't getting him anywhere. He would have to find things out for himself.

Ten o'clock seemed to be taking *forever* to arrive and Jackson had been hiding in the prop store for at least fifteen minutes. He stood with his ear to the door, listening out for Mr Greengold to arrive when he heard Mrs Jones, the cleaner, approaching, singing to herself in the corridor. Mrs Jones was always singing, to the point where everything she said had a singsong quality to it.

"Morning has broken, like the first morning!" she trilled, slightly off key. Her footsteps were getting closer. Jackson didn't want to have to explain what he was doing hiding in the half-light of the prop store. He stepped over a jumble of battered boxes to reach a pile of dust sheets that he planned to hide under.

"Blackbird has spoken!" Mrs Jones warbled behind the door.

Jackson was about to crouch down and pull the sheets over himself when he realised there was a wooden box underneath them. There was a click and the door handle turned. Jackson threw himself on the floor next to the box with the sheets on top of him. He heard the door open and light footsteps enter the room.

"Like the first bird… Now where did I put that duster?" she sang to herself as she glanced around. "Not in here."

Jackson couldn't hold his breath much longer! Luckily he could hear Mrs Jones retreating and as she closed the door behind her, he jumped up and gasped. He let the dust sheets drop and a brass clasp at the front of the box caught the light. Jackson pushed the sheets away from the box. It was like a real-life pirate's treasure chest but about a tenth of the size of one you might find on a pirate ship. It was made of strips of aged wood, stained and polished with tarnished metal corners and it looked as though it might be full of gold coins and jewels. For a moment, it crossed Jackson's mind that this could actually be the case. What if it was and there were untold riches hidden inside that could solve everything?

He knelt down and tipped the chest backwards so that he could see how the clasp worked. A cylinder of black metal on a short black chain slotted through a loop and held the clasp in place. Jackson tried to slide it open but it wasn't going to budge easily. He wrapped his fingers around it more tightly and tried again. Then pushed the cylinder from the other side to see if that worked. Just as he was about to give up, the metal gave way and started to slide a little at a time, with a grating squeak. He pulled the sheet across to dull the sound. Finally, the clasp unlocked and he could open the chest to see what was inside.

Voices suddenly echoed in the corridor. Grown up voices and footsteps walking past the door and continuing up the stairs to the office. That good-for-nothing Greengold had arrived for his meeting. Jackson looked up at the vent and heard the muffled sound of the office door being closed and then the clearer sound of his Dad's voice sounding terribly serious.

"I'll show you around properly. I know it would be good for you to see the costume department. And all the technical bits and bobs."

"And the prop store," his Mum added. "There are some valuable pieces in there."

"Yes, the more you can show me the better. We will need to work out the theatre's assets accurately. Then I can give you my estimate." Mr Greengold's voice was weak and watery. Jackson didn't trust him one little bit. "I want to go over the figures again," he continued. "Something just doesn't seem to add up."

"I just want to be really clear. We're only looking for investment, not to sell," Albert stated and Jackson heard his Dad's chair scraping as he stood up.

"I understand," Mr Greengold replied in a serious tone. "But you have a lot of repairs to do that you just can't afford. Sooner or later, it will be a matter of the health and safety of your audience. Once I've analysed things more, the figures will tell me but do you have any idea why you are losing money?"

"Maths is all just numbers to me! I prefer all the glitz and glamour," Albert attempted a laugh and fell silent for a moment. "It's always just been ok somehow. I'm sure we just need a boost in funds to tidy things up a bit to get us back on track. I've got plans for some fabulous shows in the Spring. And panto season went well last Christmas." Jackson thought his Dad was speaking like a man who was trying to convince himself.

"I want you both to know that I do have a buyer who has expressed interest. They'll make you a really good offer for the theatre and the house."

"But we can't lose our home and our livelihood. And the Merry wouldn't be, well, Merry any more. My grandfather, Billy would never forgive me. I promised him I would look after it when my father got pneumonia. And now that he isn't with us anymore, I have to keep that promise. It caused a terrible fallout in the family, my father's sister Annabel was furious. She was convinced that she should inherit the theatre and never spoke to us again. But her husband, Ernest had a terrible reputation with money, he'd even been in prison for fraud and theft and Billy insisted the Merry should never fall into his hands. I took it all on and happily so. I can't let my family down after all we've been through."

Mr Greengold remained silent during Albert's speech and there was a pause before Albert realised he was perhaps being a bit too open with his family story.

"Please don't share any of that information, Mr Greengold," Jackson heard his Mum add quietly.

"Of course, Martha, you know I'm discreet. And anyway, if you sold, you'd have enough money to buy a house, you could do something else for a living in honour of your grandfather?"

Albert suddenly sounded very small, "This theatre is my life. I don't know how to do anything else."

Jackson stood frozen to the spot. He had never known his Dad's father had a sister. Or that she had been married to a criminal. Suddenly, he heard chairs moving and he realised that he didn't have long to loiter. He looked back down at the box in his hands. Please let there be gold or jewels inside like there would be in a fairy tale, Jackson willed as he closed his eyes to make a wish and opened the lid. Please.

Jackson opened his eyes slowly and looked down into the chest. He was disappointed to find there were no gold coins and there was no big pile of jewels to be seen. Inside a curious mixture of objects lay in a jumble. Amongst them, an ornate golden oil-lamp with a long spout and also a golden crown that looked like it might fit him perfectly. Jackson shook the box a little to see what else was underneath. There may not have been gold or jewels but a beautiful wand with glass beads embedded in the design glittered in the light. And what was this underneath the lamp? Jackson reached in and picked the lamp up to see, all the while staring intently into the box. Which is why he jumped with shock when he heard a thud behind him and then a cheery voice say, "Oh hello!"

Jackson froze with his heart racing. Then finally plucked up the courage to slowly turn his head. Behind him stood a boy with a bright blue silk turban, matching blouson and pantaloons with a gold sash belt and purple velvet slippers that curled at the toes. A boy who appeared to be a Genie! Jackson was so shocked that he dropped the lamp back into the chest with a clatter as right in front of his disbelieving eyes, the Genie vanished as quickly as he had appeared. Jackson jumped to his feet, his heart pounding and looked around the room frantically, half expecting him to jump out from behind the clothes rail. Everything was still, apart from Jackson's heart, which was threatening to leap out of his chest. Where had the Genie boy gone? Had he imagined him?

A creaking noise drifted into the room and Jackson realised it was the sound of steps on the stairs.

"Let's have our walk around. We'll start in the prop store," he heard his Dad say.

Without a second's hesitation, Jackson slammed the lid of the treasure chest shut with a BANG and pulled the sheets back over the top of it. He clambered towards the door and let himself out into the corridor then scurried away from the prop store, wondering what on earth he had just seen.

CHAPTER SIX

Safely back in his bedroom, Jackson's mind was racing wildly. He paced up and down the rug in his socks hoping the rhythm of his stride might help him to make sense of things. Had he imagined the Genie? But Jackson *had* seen him, he was really there, standing in front of him, saying hello as casually as if he was always dropping by. Jackson had read about magic, about spells and wizards. He had read about genies and lamps and wishes coming true. Maybe the lamp was real, just like the one in Aladdin. Maybe the Genie had appeared from the lamp as he did in the story. Maybe. But he hadn't rubbed the lamp. Had he? Was it a trick of the light? Some sort of prank his Dad had set up for him? There was only one thing for it. He needed the theatre to himself, no hiding under sheets and holding his breath. He needed to investigate while the whole world was sleeping.

Jackson awoke with a start. He had been determined to stay awake but must have fallen asleep. He grabbed at the clock by his bed in a panic. Half past five in the morning already, his parents would be awake in an hour. Jackson slid out of bed as quickly and silently as he could. Even the 'flop' sound of the cover falling back seemed to echo around the room. He was determined to see whether what he had seen in the prop store was real. It had certainly *seemed* real. This had been his bedroom for ten years, since he was born, so he knew every creak of every floorboard and was able to silently tiptoe across the rug in a zigzag to the door as if he were avoiding a bear trap. The hallway was dark and the sound of his Dad snoring and muttering in his sleep bounced around the walls. Jackson's eyes adjusted slowly to the dim light. He knew how many steps it was from his bedroom door to the top step of the staircase (four) and how many steps there were to the bottom (twelve, or nine if you jumped the last three). He knew that his Dad's worn-out shoes would be on the mat at the bottom of the stairs and that his Mum would have straightened the address book by the telephone as she passed the hall table on her way to bed. More importantly, he knew where the key to the stage door was kept. It was on the shelf above the coat hooks. He had to stand on a chair to reach it but there it was just at his fingertips and with a couple of attempts it was in his hand. He stepped down from the chair, taking care not to make a noise and then he slipped his feet into his shoes, pulled his coat on over his pyjamas and turned the lock on the door. There was a loud and awkward click, which sounded more like a thud. Jackson froze. And waited. There was a sudden cough from upstairs and a loud clearing of a throat resonating through the floorboards. Muffled but definite. Jackson listened. Nothing. He waited a moment longer until he felt he was safe. The door opened silently thankfully and Jackson stepped out into the inky blue night, clicking the door shut behind him with such slow care that a mouse would not even have heard it.

Jackson tiptoed lightly across the cobbled courtyard. The

stage door was only a few steps away and it opened a lot more easily than the door to the house. In seconds, Jackson was inside the theatre. He locked the door behind him and switched the corridor lights on with a smile. It seemed odd to be here without actors bustling around, sweeping past in their costumes reciting their lines. Jackson realised he had never been in the theatre totally by himself before. It felt strange but also, he quickly realised, rather exciting. He headed to the prop store, switching on the light as he flew through the door. The box was under the sheets, just as he had left it. He pulled the dusty sheets to the floor and saw something on the box that he hadn't noticed earlier. The words 'The Merry Players' were stamped in black print along the side like they had been burnt into the wood. He slid the latch open with a rattle and squeak. It was easier now that it had been loosened. Inside was the pile of props he had discovered earlier that day, with the Genie's lamp resting on top. Maybe it was actually magic and if there was a Genie inside, maybe he could actually grant him a wish.

The room was silent and Jackson was beginning to think, a little eerie. He looked over his shoulder, suddenly expecting to see his Mum and Dad staring at him but finding no-one. Jackson studied the items around the lamp again. The golden crown looked exactly the right size for him. And surely the wand was magical. He noticed for the first time that there was also a tiny purple silk flower. Slowly and a little fearfully, he reached in, touching a single fingertip against the lamp but pulling his hand immediately away as if the lamp was burning hot. Nothing happened. Silence. He could feel his heart beating like a bird flapping its wings in a panic.

"Come on," he whispered to encourage himself and coaxed his hand back towards the lamp, gingerly placing his palm on it this time. Still nothing. He curled his hand around it and tightened his grip, watching closely. And with one brave sharp movement it was out of the box and at arm's length in front of him. He stared at it with wide eyes.

"Woah!" exclaimed a voice behind him. Jackson let out a yelp and dropped the lamp, causing it to tumble to the floor. "Careful!" the Genie gasped, leaning down to catch the lamp.

Jackson had his hand to his mouth and spoke through his fingers, backing towards the wall, "It's true. It really did happen."

The Genie was staring intently at the lamp. "What's true?" he asked, studying his reflection and raising his eyebrows in approval.

"You're... real," Jackson stammered.

The Genie looked down at himself. "Yes," he smiled, "Why wouldn't I be?"

"But I didn't even rub the lamp, where did you come from?"

"I'm not sure, one minute I was on stage and now I'm here. And I'm wearing this costume... What's going on?" The Genie was looking around the room with great curiosity and more than a little confusion. "Shouldn't I get back on stage? We're in the middle of rehearsing..."

"*On stage?* But you *must* have come from the lamp. You're a *Genie.*"

"Oh no, I'm not an *actual* Genie. This is just a costume, silly!" he smiled, flapping the sleeves of his blouson.

"What?" Jackson was feeling a little braver now and stopped cowering.

"I'm not a *Genie*, I've played him in a play before, you know?

37

I'm an actor, a boy, like you." Seeing Jackson's blank expression he continued, "I played the Genie. In Aladdin. With this lamp. And this costume. Who do you play?" Jackson continued to gaze at him. He was maybe the same age as him.

"I don't play anything. I'm Jackson." The Genie looked at him blankly so he continued. "I'm Albert and Martha's son." Still nothing. "They own the theatre!"

"No, no, Constance and Billy own the theatre. They were just on the stage with me," the Genie stated assuredly. "Who are Albert and Martha?"

Jackson's mind was reeling. "Constance and Billy are my great-grandparents. They don't own the theatre anymore."

"They do! They're directing the play we're doing." The Genie was looking at Jackson as though he was slightly crazy.

Jackson couldn't decide if he felt amazed or irritated. "But you appeared from the lamp!"

"Did I?"

"Well, not exactly," Jackson realised. "But you appeared when I took it out of the box."

"Right," the Genie nodded, clearly confused.

"Is that what usually happens?"

"I've no idea."

"I mean… It seems like you were on the stage… With my great-grandparents. And now you're here. With me. Like you travelled in time? Is that right? Did you?" Jackson said peering into the box and holding out his hand, "Pass me the lamp."

The boy passed Jackson the lamp, still looking baffled. Jackson took a deep breath and plunged it back into the box. Immediately he found himself alone. He stared at the lamp, unable to widen his eyes any more. He lifted it again, less scared this time. And 'TING!' there he was, the Genie, or boy or whatever he was.

"So what happened? Where did you go?" Jackson asked eagerly.

The Genie reached forwards and took the lamp from Jackson lightly. He turned it slowly around in his hands, gazing at it from every angle. "I was back on stage, exactly where I was before, in my other costume, right in the middle of my line." He smiled confidently. "I picked it up, no problem, don't worry. But… How?"

"I have no idea…" There was a pause as both boys stared at the lamp. "It IS magic!" they chorused.

"Does that mean *YOU* are magic then?" Jackson ventured. "I mean, can you actually grant wishes, like in stories?"

"Of course!" the Genie replied confidently, getting into character. "In fact, you've got three of them!" he grinned as he suddenly turned his back on Jackson, looping his fingers through the handle of the lamp and admiring his reflection in a dusty full-length mirror. Jackson watched him curiously. The Genie span back around to face him, "Go on, anything!"

Jackson decided to go along with him. "Well, I already know one."

"Yes?"

"I wish I could save the theatre so we don't have to sell it and so we don't have to move."

"What? You're selling the theatre? Do Constance and Billy know?" the Genie said in alarm.

"No. I mean, I don't know!" Jackson exclaimed, confused again. "I don't think so. Can you help or not?"

"Of course. Right." The Genie stated, hesitating for a moment before closing his eyes and throwing his head back dramatically. "Magic and tricks and treats abound! Make this theatre safe and sound!"

Then he muttered something under his breath that sounded a little like 'Alacazam' and a little like 'Abracadabra' and made a sharp 'whooosh' sound through his teeth as he waved his arm through the air theatrically. He opened his eyes again and they both waited a moment before he added, "Of course, it's better when I'm on stage. And I usually have some confetti handy that I throw up in the air. It's only paper but I like to pretend it's golden."

He smiled broadly at Jackson who was wondering whether he dared ask the question that was on his mind. He decided to be brave, "So, have you *actually* just granted my wish? Is the theatre saved?"

"Yes, my friend, it is," replied the Genie as he grinned from ear to ear.

"Wow. Simple as that?" Jackson looked around. The props room looked exactly as it had done. The props from recent shows were still on the shelves, the box of old scripts was still stuffed in the corner and the mirror still needed cleaning.

"And for your second wish?" the Genie asked seeming slightly smug, once again admiring himself and smoothing his eyebrows down with a forefinger.

Jackson wanted to believe his wish had been granted but how could he know for sure? He couldn't *see* any difference. He couldn't *see* whether the theatre was out of danger. Hadn't he just said he wasn't really a Genie anyway, just an actor in costume? He thought quickly. He needed to wish for something he could *see*. But if the wishes did come true, he didn't want to waste a wish.

"I know!" he grinned, an idea coming to him. "Follow me!"

and with that he headed out of the prop store, the Genie following quickly behind, skidding out into the corridor on his velvety slippers.

CHAPTER SEVEN

In the wings, it was as dark as the night. Jackson groped around to find the switch. One click and a dim bulb lit up, giving him enough light to see the metal lever that would turn on the front of house lights. With one hefty pull, the theatre was lit up and Jackson ducked through the drape to see the effect on the stage, with the Genie still skidding along behind him. It was dazzling. The red seats stood to attention in front of them. The huge curtains on either side of the stage swept down dramatically. With only himself and the Genie on it, the stage seemed immense.

The Genie strode confidently across the floorboards, "Oh! I love being on the sta..." Suddenly he stopped in his tracks. "Goodness, what's happened to this place?"

"It just needs a few repairs that's all," Jackson responded defensively. "That's what I..."

"Alacazam!" the Genie suddenly blurted out loudly, once again distracted. "That's always an audience favourite. All the other children shout it out and I throw confetti onto them. You should see their faces, *total* amazement."

He looked wistfully across the empty rows of seats. Jackson approached him, looking out in the same direction, picturing the confetti falling in front of him.

"So you've been on this stage a lot?" Jackson finally asked, breaking the silence.

The Genie turned to him quickly, "Of course." And with that, he jumped off the stage, into the stalls and started to walk purposefully towards the back of the auditorium. Jackson jumped down with a thud and followed him.

"I've done loads of shows here," the Genie replied matter-of-factly, storming ahead and then turning around so abruptly that Jackson crashed into him. "So what's your second wish?" he asked as he sat down in one of the threadbare seats, swinging his legs back and forth as he looked at Jackson with interest.

"These seats," Jackson stated, "And the carpet and paint on the walls. I'd like them all tidied up, please, so this place looks totally renewed. If we've been saved…"

The Genie interrupted, "Which you have."

"Then we're going to have even bigger audiences and more money coming in so I don't want my parents to have to spend the whole lot on cleaning this place up. So, yes, I'd like the whole building to look sparkly, shiny and new."

The Genie jumped up and was practically running back to the stage, still clutching the lamp with an iron grip.

"Where are you going now?" exclaimed Jackson, the Genie was beginning to rub him up the wrong way.

"I want to do this properly!"

In a moment, the Genie was standing back up by the footlights with Jackson watching from the front row like an audience member waiting for the show to start. The Genie cleared his throat and looked Jackson directly in the eye.

"A second wish to make things new, I will make your wish come true!" As he said the word 'true' the Genie span around and twirled his arm like a dancer. "Alacadabrazam!" he exclaimed and once again blew the word 'whoosh' through his teeth, throwing imaginary confetti out as he did so. Then, there was silence.

Jackson dared to look around him as the Genie bowed, a long sweeping bow. "I thank you," he grinned and looked at Jackson eagerly awaiting his applause.

"But nothing's changed!" Jackson blurted out as he stood up. The Genie's grin started to fade. "It's all the same. The seats are still old and tatty, the carpets are still worn, the walls still desperately need painting! The wish didn't work. Which means the first wish didn't work either. The theatre's not saved at all."

"Well, I did say you have to use your imagination," the Genie tutted and rolled his eyes.

"No you didn't."

"Oh. Well, I meant to."

"You *meant* to? That's helpful. You're not a Genie at all. You're just a boy, just like me. You can't grant wishes or do magic. You can't save the theatre, just like *I* can't save the theatre. You may as well go back to where you came from."

The Genie sat down, his legs dangling over the edge of the stage.

"I told you I wasn't *really* a Genie. What did you expect? Your wishes to come true?" he half laughed but immediately stopped as he saw Jackson's serious expression.

"Yes," said Jackson as he got up and stomped back to the prop store leaving the Genie unusually speechless.

Jackson looked about miserably as the Genie followed him

into the room. The box was still open as he'd left it, with the other props inside in a pile.

"Here," the Genie said holding the lamp out in front of him. "Take it. I'm sorry I can't grant your wishes." He looked at Jackson sideways and added a little sulkily, "I did say you just need a little imagination…"

Jackson glared at the Genie and snatched the lamp quickly in case he changed his mind again. In one swoop, he grabbed the box by the lid and dropped the lamp into it. Right in front of Jackson's eyes the Genie vanished. Totally. Gone. Like a light going out. Jackson looked around, expecting him to jump out and say he was only joking. What he hadn't noticed was that as he tipped the box, the tiny purple silk flower that he had spotted earlier had fallen out and drifted softly to the floor. All of a sudden, Jackson heard a new voice behind him.

"Woah! Good morrow, dear boy, what vision are you? A pixie or an imp?"

Jackson turned his head with a gulp and looked at the new arrival with an open-mouth trying to work out what had just happened. The new voice belonged to a waifish girl with a grin as wide as her face. She spoke again, "Or a fairy?"

She looked boyish with choppy, cropped hair and a very mischievous twinkle in her eye.

"I'm a boy," Jackson stuttered. "Who are you?"

"You should know me! I'm that playful sprite, Puck."

"Did you come from the lamp too?" Jackson spluttered as Puck walked across the room on tiptoes like a tightrope walker. She was wearing green tights and a tunic of sorts, tied around the middle with a piece of string.

"I don't *think* so. I'm not sure how I got here. Do you know?" Before Jackson could respond, Puck trailed off as she grinned and suddenly leapt down to scoop something from the ground, "Ah ha! My flower! Trickery will abound, where this flower is found!" She span around and landed with a little jump.

Jackson looked more closely at the flower. "The purple flower! It was in the box. That must be where you came from!"

Puck leant playfully towards the box with the flower in the palm of her hand, "It is a box? Or is it a trunk? Like the trunk of an elephant?"

As soon as the flower crossed the threshold of the box, Puck disappeared in front of Jackson's eyes and the flower drifted silently down onto the remaining props.

He tingled with excitement, all the way from his head to his toes. "It's ALL the props in the box, not just the lamp," he whispered to himself.

Jackson retrieved the flower from the treasure chest, picking up the lamp with it, suddenly feeling that he wanted the Genie to be there with him to see this. Puck was once again standing in front of him, looking mischievous and didn't seem at all affected by her return to the box.

The Genie looked at Jackson and a smile spread across his face, "I knew you'd forgive me!" He leant towards him to hug him and even though Jackson kept his arms firmly by his sides, he couldn't help warming to his new friend a little. "Ah hello!" the Genie exclaimed to Puck. "Weren't you just on stage too?"

"I was," she replied, suddenly looking a little confused. Jackson twirled the flower between his fingers. It wasn't even real, he thought to himself, it was made of silk with pieces shaped into petals.

"Which play are you in?" Jackson asked.

"Ah, now this, I know. In this costume, I'm in the Merry

Players' production of A Midsummer Night's Dream by the Bard himself, William Shakespeare."

Jackson looked between them. "I've never even heard of the Merry Players and I've lived at this theatre all my life. We put on Shakespeare plays sometimes but I can barely understand them."

"We only do a short version," Puck replied, "I just say the lines I'm told to say so it doesn't seem too complicated to me. And it's a magical story with a King and a Queen and fairies and a man with a head like a donkey."

The Genie chipped in, "Aladdin is set in a mysterious far-off land with a poor boy and a princess and I appear as if by magic from that very lamp."

Jackson instinctively held the lamp just a little tighter.

"Of course, the audience have to use a little imagination..." the Genie continued.

Puck was nodding her head and agreeing whole-heartedly, "Oh yes, they have to use their imaginations."

Jackson watched and now that he had calmed down a little, he could see past the distraction of their costumes. They were just children playing characters. They were actors! The Genie even had a smudged, curly moustache drawn on his face with black pencil and Puck's cropped hair was teased up in points with hair wax.

"What are your real names?" Jackson asked curiously.

"My real name is Sonny but we have a bit of a game. As soon as we're in costume, we use our character's name," the Genie explained lightly, fiddling with an ornament that he had found on one of the shelves.

"Like my name's Sophia," Puck said, picking up where the Genie had left off. Somehow, she didn't look like a Sophia at all. "But as soon as I'm dressed in this, I'm Puck. Constance says it helps us to *really* get into character. And it does. It's fun!"

"I like that," Jackson replied, thinking how nice it must be to really escape into being a character. He watched as the Genie picked up some trinkets from the shelf. A glass, a pair of binoculars, a watch. Seeing the watch, Jackson suddenly realised he had absolutely no idea what time it was and with some concern rushed out into the corridor to check the time on the old black and white clock that hung on the wall backstage. Twenty past six? Twenty past six! His parents would be awake any minute now. He rushed back into the prop store.

"I'm sorry, I'll bring you back I promise!" he said suddenly and as the Genie and Puck looked at him in surprise as Jackson dropped the lamp and the flower back into the box. In a heartbeat, he was alone again. He glanced at the other props, burning with curiosity about whether they might also summon other actors. But there wasn't time. It would be too risky to investigate another prop now with only minutes left to get back into bed before his Mum and Dad woke up. And that was assuming that the other props would be magical too. Maybe it was just Genie and Puck who appeared? Whatever was happening, it was magic and he was willing to take whatever magic he could get. He slowly lowered the lid of the box back down and noticed the writing on the side again, 'The Merry Players'. He would have to find out more about them from his parents. Jackson leant down and reluctantly but quickly pulled the sheets back over the chest. He turned the light off and closed the door behind him as he headed backstage to turn the theatre lights off. And then he was out of the stage door and turning the key in the lock with his head full of excitement and thoughts about Puck and the Genie on stage with his great-grandparents.

The indigo night sky was slowly lightening into dawn, the pinpoint stars disappearing into the light and everything around him felt fresh and clear. For a moment, Jackson could remember what it felt like before all the trouble had started. Before money had been such a problem, before Mr Greengold and the Weasel had appeared. Jackson sighed and crept back in to the house, being careful not to make a sound. He placed the key on the shelf with more stealth than a fox and avoided the creaky floorboards as he sneaked up the stairs. As he climbed back under his bedcovers he heard his parents' bedroom door open and his Mum crept down the stairs, trying not to wake him.

CHAPTER EIGHT

At the breakfast table Jackson was yawning.

"Not enough sleep?" his Mum asked. "What have I told you about reading until all hours?"

Jackson crunched on a piece of toast with strawberry jam and made a 'hmm' sound. Little did she know that there were enchanted props in a box in the prop store and both of the children that they summoned were convinced that they could perform magic! He watched his Mum as she poured tea into a cup. He had also been thinking about his great uncle Ernest who had been in prison and was desperate to ask about him but knew that if he did, he would have to confess that he'd been eavesdropping. So he asked another question that was on his mind. "Who are the Merry Players?" Martha waited for him to elaborate so he continued, "I saw it written on the side of a kind of treasure chest in the prop store."

"I know the one you mean, it was your great-grandma's." His Mum placed the teapot gently down on the kitchen worktop as she spoke and carried her tea over to the table to sit opposite her son. She curled both hands around the cup, "Your Dad can tell you all about them."

On cue, Albert walked into the kitchen, yawning and looking dark around his eyes. "Dad can tell you all about who?"

"The Merry Players," Jackson said through a mouthful of toast.

"Ah!" a smile spread across Albert's face, "Your great-grandad told me all about the Merry Players. They were your great-grandmother Constance's creation. She used to run a little theatre club for local children on a Sunday afternoon and they'd put on shows for their parents. All sorts of plays and musicals."

Jackson had stopped eating and was transfixed as his Dad absent-mindedly picked up an apple from the fruit bowl and bit into it. "What plays did they put on?"

"I don't know," Albert replied, through a mouthful of apple. "I guess things like Aladdin and Cinderella."

"And A Midsummer Night's Dream?" asked Jackson eagerly.

"Maybe," Albert smiled. "There's a box of their props still in the prop store somewhere. My grandmother kept something from each of her favourite plays." He stopped and looked at his half-eaten apple. "I think there was a gold lamp in there, from a production of Aladdin. Not real gold, of course. If it was I'd be cashing it in!" He stopped for a moment, realising he was being too open with his son. "Better get on, I've got business to attend to."

Once Martha had gone to help Albert in the theatre, Jackson ran up the stairs two at a time. He was already planning to go back to the prop store that night, when he wouldn't be interrupted to see what else the Merry Players' treasure chest held. But in the meantime, it was obvious to him that the Merry Theatre was in trouble and he'd had an idea about how he could help. Mr Greengold had said they needed to work out how much the theatre was worth and his Dad had mentioned thinking about selling the lamp. They needed money. Jackson picked up his money box from his bedside table and opened it to shake the contents out onto the bedspread. Three gold coins dropped with a plop onto the bed. It wasn't going to get him very far. He looked at the shelves full of books in front of him, running his eyes along their colourful spines. All of them meant so much to him but they would mean a lot to someone else too, they were worth something. He would sell them, every last one and save his home. He would save the Merry Theatre.

Without wasting a moment, he started pulling books down from the shelves. His new collection of plays, his well-loved picture books, thick well-thumbed novels, comics with torn edges and annuals full of animals and history. He stacked them carefully in two, tall, wavering piles trying to ignore how sad he felt at the thought of losing each and every one. He would set up a stall in front of the theatre and sell them all, he decided, placing them quickly into a cardboard box before he could change his mind. Then he rolled up the rug from the floor and slung it over his shoulder before picking the box up, staggering out of his room and swaying dangerously down the stairs.

Outside the front of the Merry Theatre, Jackson let the box drop to the ground and shook his hands to recover from carrying it. The rug rolled off of his shoulder and landed with a gentle thud on the pavement. Jackson set up shop next to the entrance and fanned the books out on the rug. He was so focused on selling his books that it took him a moment to realise that something was different as he looked up. Then he realised what it was. The sign. The sign that had been ornately carved out of dark wood by Jackson's great-grandfather, Billy, with the lines and curves of the letters painted in gold. THE MERRY THEATRE it read. Except it didn't because the sign had disappeared. The sign had been stolen! And not only that but the doors of the theatre had been painted black, with big streaks slopped on back and forth and trails of inky paint dripping down the frame. And as Jackson looked around him, he noticed a splash of black paint on the road.

Jackson knelt down on the rug and urgently gathered his books back into the box. As he staggered back to his feet, across the road, he spotted Harry Cuthbert approaching. He must be on his way in for rehearsals or out to run some errands in town. He would know what to do, Jackson thought.

"Harry!" he called out.

Harry didn't hear him and hadn't seen him yet. He didn't look at all as cheery and chirpy as he always did when he was backstage. Jackson called again and waited for Harry to turn towards the Merry Theatre to cross the road but was shocked to see none other than the Weasel step from the shadows of the scaffolding, his hair swept back like an oil slick, his pointy nose looking particularly pointy and unpleasant. The Weasel weaselled his way towards Harry. To Jackson's surprise, Harry stopped and shook the Weasel's hand and the two men disappeared under the scaffolding and out of sight. Without another thought Jackson grabbed the box of books, dragging the rug behind him, wondering how on earth Harry even *knew* the villain across the road, let alone why he would be meeting with him.

Inside the Merry, Albert and Martha were in their office deep in conversation. Jackson had flung his box of books and the rug on the floor outside the backstage door and run down the corridor. He appeared at the door, out of breath.

"Someone's stolen the theatre sign!" he blurted out. "And slopped paint all over the doors!"

Albert was already half way across the room before Jackson could finish what he was saying. He charged straight across the stage, the soles of his shoes thudding on the floorboards, with Martha and Jackson trying to keep up with him. They zigzagged through the seats in the stalls and into the foyer. Albert unlocked the front door and flung it open, striding into the street and looking up.

"What on earth?" he exclaimed, open-mouthed, touching the black paint on the doors to see if it was still wet.

"Who would…" Martha trailed off in disbelief looking around.

"And I saw Harry going into the old town hall too. I called out to him but he didn't…" Jackson stopped as his Dad carried on talking. He wasn't listening.

"The paint's still wet," stated Albert firmly, looking at the black on his fingertips. "That means this only happened this morning."

"We've got some other paint somewhere, I'll paint over it," Martha soothed. "We can make a temporary sign, until we can afford a new one. I know it won't be…"

"How can it be the same?" Albert's voice wobbled as he spoke. "Billy carved that sign himself. It's part of the theatre. What kind of…" Albert turned and stormed back inside with Martha following.

Jackson watched the backs of his parents, knowing it was pointless trying to tell them what he knew. He needed to try to find out what Harry was up to. He felt braver this time, ducking under the tarpaulin, not really caring who saw. But each window was in darkness, the heavy curtains drawn so Jackson couldn't see inside. Then, just as he was about to give up, he saw it. A tiny smear of wet black paint on the door handle.

CHAPTER NINE

Jackson lay awake in the moonlight for a second night, listening out for his parents to go to bed. It had been a tense evening backstage and Jackson had tried his best to keep out of the way. Emma had telephoned only an hour before she was due on stage to say that she had come down with a mysterious illness and would not be able to perform that night. This led to a fraught forty minutes in which Albert had to prepare Emma's understudy, Louisa, to perform the lead female role for the first time. It was only when Louisa put on Emma's costume that they realised the dress was far too big for her and Martha had to spend a frantic ten minutes pinning her into it to make it look like it was meant to be hers. And then Harry arrived late, looking ruffled and he then kept fluffing his lines which was most unlike him. Jackson just knew it was because of his meeting across the road.

Downstairs, the front door of the house swooshed gently across the doormat. He heard his Dad muttering with his Mum and then the subdued sound of serious voices followed by slow plodding footsteps up the stairs and his parents shushing each other as they passed his bedroom door. A short while later, the gentle sound of snoring resonated through the wall and

Jackson slid out of bed just as he had done the night before. He knew to be careful with the front door this time and managed to escape silently across the courtyard and in through the stage door, locking it behind him and heading straight to the prop store. The room was just as he had left it and as he pushed the sheets back from the treasure chest he felt his pulse quicken with anticipation. With the lid up, the contents stared back at him. He wanted to see what other secrets the props held. He picked his way around the lamp and the silk flower and reached cautiously for the wand.

Just as quickly as the Genie and Puck had appeared, there in front of his eyes, a rosy-cheeked girl materialised.

"Ta-dah!" she exclaimed, blinking in shock, then noticing Jackson. "What just happened? Oh my goodness, the others told me this had happened to them but I didn't think they were telling the truth! Are you Jackson?"

Jackson, a little more prepared this time, stepped forward to greet her warmly. "Yes!" he smiled and as he did so he noticed what she was wearing. A slightly shabby, faded frock and cloak. She was straightening a silver grey wig that sat lopsided on her head.

"Sorry, I'm not sure who you are," Jackson apologised.

"I know, this costume is terrible. I played the Fairy God-mother in it. I asked Constance if we could make something more sparkly but this was all we had," the girl replied turning to look in the mirror and adjusting her ill-fitting wig a little more. "There," she said once she was satisfied. She turned back to Jackson and he held back a giggle. The wig looked nothing short of ridiculous.

"I thought you were the Prince first of all but then I realised what had happened," the girl said with a glint in her eye glancing at the wand in Jackson's hand. Jackson was a bit confused and not for the first time in the past few days. He held the wand a little more tightly.

"It was the wand," he responded, "You know… It brought you here."

"So it really is magic then?" she said suddenly holding her hand out for the wand. "I mean, I always pretend it is. But it *actually* is!"

"Yes. But you can't *really* grant wishes. You're just an actor. I mean, the wand somehow brought you here through time but it's not *actually* magic," Jackson said flatly, realising he wasn't really making sense because if the wand *had* brought her here, it clearly *was* magic.

The girl looked understandably confused, "But… I have to believe I can grant wishes when I'm in this costume. Constance says, we have to fully be our characters, otherwise what's the point?"

Jackson wanted to get to *his* point more quickly than he had done with the Genie.

"Show me then. Make something magical happen," he dared her, leaning back confidently as she stared back defiantly.

"Right, I will. You want to go to the ball? You shall go to the ball!" With that the Fairy Godmother turned and strutted out of the room dramatically.

"Where are you going?" Jackson called after her and then a little more snappily, "I don't want to go to a ball!"

What was it with these props? Why was everyone they conjured up so unruly and uncontrollable? And why did they all want to grant wishes? Jackson was beginning to wonder why he was bothering to find out more about the treasure chest.

Was he just letting it distract him from the fact he should be thinking of a way to save the theatre? Headstrong characters magically appearing wasn't very helpful at all. He clutched the wand and followed the girl determinedly out into the corridor, just catching sight of her cloak as she swept into the wardrobe room.

When Jackson caught up with the Fairy Godmother, she was rapidly rifling through a rail of costumes. The hangers clinked against each other as she pushed them across one by one, saying under her breath, "No… No… No…" And then triumphantly, "Ah ha!"

She lifted an outfit from the rail. A princely-looking embroidered velvet jacket and matching knee-length trousers.

"Ta-dah!" she beamed at Jackson and he wondered if this was perhaps her favourite expression. "Your outfit, my Prince! You shall go to the ball!" she added, thrusting it towards him enthusiastically. "But beware, if you do not return it by midnight, it will turn back into rags!"

"It's already past midnight. And it didn't start off as rags," said Jackson dryly, replacing the costume onto the rail.

The Fairy Godmother looked dejected, "Well, there's no need to be so ungrateful. I was just granting your wish."

"I didn't *wish* to go to a ball. And that isn't granting a wish, that's just finding an outfit on a rail," Jackson could feel himself getting more and more irritated.

"How about this one?" The Fairy Godmother had lifted another jacket-trouser combination from the rail and was holding it up against him. Jackson raised his eyebrows sarcastically and she replaced it slowly, daring to ask, "What do you want to wish for then?"

"You wouldn't understand," Jackson snapped and left the room, heading back towards the prop store. He wanted to put the wand back in the chest and to get rid of this supposed Fairy Godmother. He heard her running behind him, "Come on, tell me. What use am I as a Fairy Godmother if I don't at least listen to people's wishes? Tell me. There must be something I can do!"

She was nothing if not persistent. Jackson turned to face her and seeing the pleading look on her face, felt a little sorry for her. He could see some strands of hair poking out from the rather dishevelled silver wig and noticed that the dress she was wearing was a little big for her. He thought about how Louisa had had to go on stage at the last minute that very night and how brave she had been to step into Emma's role with only an hour's warning. He thought about what it took to get onto the stage at all and suddenly wanted to give this girl a chance to believe she could play the role and make wishes come true. And besides, Jackson really wanted to believe that there was a reason that he had found the props and that his discovery could help him. He just wasn't sure exactly how.

"Come on then," he said as he handed her the wand and led the way to the stage.

Jackson pulled the lever down and flooded the stage with light. The Fairy Godmother stood beside him holding the drape back and staring open-mouthed at the sight of the set that was still in place from the night's performance. Close up you could see the flat hand-painted strokes but from the stalls it looked like the three-dimensional façade of a grand stone house. They walked out across the floorboards without talking, their footsteps tip-tapping and sounding a lot louder than they actually were in the stillness. The Fairy Godmother stared up into the rafters where other pieces of set hung heavily on ropes, ready to be lowered down on cue. She looked out to the seats, just as the Genie had done the night before and waved her magic wand silently, running her lines through her head. Jackson watched her curiously.

"You must be a brilliant actor to get asked to do such a big role," Jackson said kindly.

"I'm not brilliant. There were all these people staring at me. I found it all pretty scary to be honest."

"Then why did you do it? I'm terrified of being on stage in front of all those people," Jackson was thinking about his own sense of fear. A fear of people looking at him with wide eyes. A fear of messing up and of getting things wrong. A fear of being laughed at.

"I don't know really," the Fairy Godmother replied. "I just like being someone else and I like dressing up in costumes." She swished her skirt around her legs.

"And you like granting wishes, don't you?"

His new friend's eyes lit up, "Yes, I love making dreams come true!" She waved her wand and threw her arm out to the side, making her wig slip a little as she did so. "I got so excited about that bit, it stopped me worrying so much about all those people watching."

"Do you want to grant me a wish then?"

"Just name it and I'll make it come true straight away!" She blinked at him expectantly.

Jackson had learnt his lesson from the Genie. This girl *playing* at being the Fairy Godmother wouldn't be able to transform the auditorium, to mend the chairs and paint the walls or to stop whoever it was vandalising the theatre, with a wave of her wand. But perhaps she could help him with something else. What he really wanted to wish for was courage. Maybe the Fairy Godmother could help him with that. After all, she had confessed to being scared when she first stepped on the stage too. And now it wasn't just on the stage that Jackson felt scared. He was starting to feel more and more scared about everything. Scared about the Merry Theatre running out of money and closing down. Scared about what would happen if they lost their home. Scared about who the Weasel and string-haired man were and what they were up to. Scared about why Harry was having secret meetings. Jackson didn't want to feel scared. Maybe if he started with not being so scared on stage any more, it would help him to not be so scared about everything else. He turned to face his new Fairy Godmother.

"I wish... that you would give me courage to perform on stage again," he announced and waited for her reaction.

A smile spread across her face, "I will grant your wishes, one and all! You shall go to the Prince's ball!" she said in a sing-songy voice. Then seeing Jackson's puzzled expression, continued, "And by that, I mean, I shall give you courage! Sorry, I just like saying my lines. Right, come and stand here."

With that, she led him by the hand to the middle of the stage and positioned him so that he was facing out into the darkness. He stood frozen, waiting for instruction as she faced him. Somewhere faintly he thought he could hear someone laughing.

"This is what Constance taught us."

The mention of his great-grandmother's name made him pay attention. "Wow, really?"

"Yes! Ok, shake your arms a bit, like this. And then swing them around like this." She waved her arms and swung them around her, gathering momentum. Jackson copied her and rolled his shoulders.

"Now, jump up and down!" She was now jumping around like a frog on springs and he was wondering quite how this was going to help him to gain the confidence to save his home but copied her nevertheless. He wanted to learn lessons from his great-grandmother. In a funny way he was starting to enjoy himself.

"Now make a face like this." The Fairy Godmother stuck her tongue out and waggled her hands next to her ears, then burst out laughing.

Jackson self-consciously copied her and found himself smirking at how ridiculous he felt. He copied her as she hopped around in a circle on one leg and galloped up and down the stage pretending to be on a horse. Then suddenly, she started shouting made up words out into the stalls. And not just made up words. Ridiculous, outlandish words.

"Cakeshoes! Bananasky! Chickensocks! Treeface! You try!" she spun around to look at her pupil.

Jackson was standing totally still. "I can't. It's silly." He was suddenly thrown back to that moment, hearing that one laugh from the crowd. Then another, then another. Feeling the redness of his blushes creep up his face.

"It's only me here," the Fairy Godmother said gently.

"It's not that easy." Jackson shrank down and sat on the floor cross-legged, leaning his elbow on his leg and sinking his chin into his hands. He could feel tears stinging his eyes.

The Fairy Godmother walked over to him softly and sat down next to him. "What's the matter?"

"I thought I loved being on stage," he said quietly.

"Why don't you?"

"I was in a show. My first show. My Mum and Dad trusted me with the part. And on the last night, I forgot a line. And everyone laughed at me. And I mean *everyone*. The whole audience. They just thought I was ridiculous. I let everyone down."

The Fairy Godmother put her hand gently on his shoulder. "I'm sure they weren't laughing at you. Maybe they were trying to laugh with you? Constance says laughing at yourself is one of the most important things you can learn. She always tells us to laugh when we get things wrong or feel embarrassed. That's why she gets us to shout the silliest thing we can think of. To get used to laughing at ourselves." Jackson looked up at his new friend through tearful eyes.

"I'll show you…" She jumped to her feet and walked away from him towards the front of the stage. Silhouetted in the light, she shouted as loudly as she could, "Cakeshoes!" and then started giggling at herself.

Jackson found himself smiling a little despite himself. With her wonky wig and dress that was slightly too big, she looked pretty ridiculous. And her laugh was infectious.

"Go on…" she span round and looked at him with a big grin.

"Umm… Ok. Cakeshoes," Jackson said reluctantly. He slowly got up and looked down at his feet. "Cakeshoes," he repeated feeling a little silly.

"Cakeshoes!" the Fairy Godmother shouted back with a twinkle in her eye.

"Cakeshoes!" His voice was a little louder. The more he said it, the sillier it sounded. Very slowly a smile started to form on his face. "Cakeshoes!" he shouted again as he edged towards the front of the stage feeling a little less foolish. "CaaaaaaakeSHOES!"

He shouted it over and over. Suddenly noticing that he was actually enjoying himself, in the floodlights, with an audience, albeit just one girl and one he had conjured up from a wand at that. He imagined each and every seat in the auditorium being full and for a reason he couldn't quite explain, it didn't feel quite as bad as it had done before. The Fairy Godmother was laughing so much that she fell to the floor and lay on her back trying to get her breath back.

Jackson carried on shouting, "Magicmoons! Blanketpops!" while she giggled uncontrollably until Jackson, too, fell to the floor and lay on his back with a big grin on his face.

"See?" the Fairy Godmother asked, looking up at the lights and scenery.

"Yes... I do," Jackson said slowly, realising for the first time that something was just a little bit different and that he suddenly felt just a little bit less afraid. He propped himself up on his elbows and looked across the stage, "Thank you, Fairy Godmother."

CHAPTER TEN

Feeling more positive than he had done in days, Jackson jumped up managing to make the Fairy Godmother jump in the process. She promptly sat bolt upright and got to her feet.

"Let's see who else is in the treasure chest!" Jackson strode across the stage with a new found confidence, followed by his enthusiastic companion.

Back in the prop store, he knelt by the box. "Let's see who else can come through the props."

With that, Jackson reached in and grabbed the golden crown that perched at the top of the pile. The Fairy Godmother stared, her eyes like saucers. Surely it would summon a prince or a king? As Jackson lifted the crown out of the chest, there he stood. A boy standing in a regal pose wearing a frilly, white shirt, black knee length trousers with a gold buckle belt, white tights and buckled shoes that matched his belt. He looked down at his outfit and then patted himself on the head and began to look around in a bit of a panic. Finally noticing Jackson and exclaiming, "My crown! How dare you steal the Prince's crown! En garde!"

Suddenly he was holding a wooden sword aloft and waving it at Jackson who jumped backwards. He charged towards him and gave Jackson no alternative but to run from the room.

The two boys ran down the corridor at full speed, their feet thudding along the floorboards, Jackson clinging to the crown. The Fairy Godmother, not having really understood how the treasure chest worked, thought it best to pop the wand back in there for safe keeping before following the boys. So before she knew it... 'TING!' She had disappeared.

Jackson ran around the back of the stage towards the door to the stalls and just had time to slam it behind him. He continued to run along the side of the stalls. Only the stage lights were on so the rows of seats were shrouded in darkness.

Jackson's eyes adjusted quickly as he aimed for the furthest possible corner, shouting back as he went, "Stop chasing me! I didn't steal your crown!"

He heard rattling as the Prince grappled with the door-handle and called out into the darkness. "Where are you? You coward! You scoundrel! Come and face your fate!"

The Prince waved his sword from side to side as he crept along the rows trying to spot his rival. Jackson crouched behind the back row, out of sight.

"Look! Just stay still for a moment and listen to me!"

"Give me my crown back!" the Prince demanded.

"It's just a prop! It belongs to the theatre, not you," Jackson shouted back.

"Come out you scaredy-cat!"

That was it. After the lesson he had learnt about courage from the Fairy Godmother, he was not in the mood to be mocked.

"BISCUITBOOTS! I am NOT a scaredy-cat!" Jackson couldn't help himself, he jumped up and waved the crown at the Prince. "You can't catch me!" he teased and watched as the Prince looked around frantically and then spied him at the back of the room. The Prince began running towards him at great speed still brandishing the sword. Jackson quickly ducked into one of the rows. The Prince was quick and scuttled along the row and down the middle aisle with surprising speed. Jackson jostled along, trying not to bash his legs on the flipped up seats. With his adversary gathering pace behind him, he changed direction quickly and aimed for the stage, taking the steps in one leap and spinning round.

"Just listen to me for a minute!" Jackson demanded, staring at the Prince who was unnervingly close to striking him with the sword. "Here! Have the crown! But give me the sword first."

The Prince stopped in his tracks and as he considered Jackson's offer, Jackson saw his chance and snatched the sword from his rival whilst keeping a firm hold of the crown. The Prince, realising he was being somewhat out-foxed, relented and smoothed his ruffled hair. He was pristine-looking. Jackson could see why he would be given the Princely role.

"I'm Jackson, I live here at the theatre," Jackson offered.

"I'm Prince Charming," the Prince said sulkily. "Well, I am when I'm wearing my crown."

"So you know the Fairy Godmother?" Jackson asked, ignoring the crown comment.

"Of course! I know all the Merry Players," he pronounced puffing his chest up with pride. "And I've been cast as the Prince twice."

All of a sudden, there was HUGE CLUNK sound. Jackson looked around alarmed. The Prince, unnerved by Jackson's reaction, also looked around. Was it the prop store door? The stage door? The office door? The front door?

"Who is it?" the Prince whispered and Jackson SSSHH-HUSHED him, standing stock-still and listening carefully. Another click.

"It's coming from the lobby," Jackson whispered. "Quick." He led the way, tiptoeing bravely down the stage steps and along the middle aisle towards the double doors that led to the foyer. He held the Prince's wooden sword out in front of him, not altogether sure what he was going to do with it. The Prince cowered uncharacteristically, creeping along closely behind. There was another noise, like something being dragged along the carpet. As Jackson stopped suddenly, the Prince walked straight into his back causing both boys to jump. Jackson turned to look at his new companion and whispered through gritted teeth.

"Aren't Princes supposed to be brave?"

"You've got my sword!"

"Sssshush!" Jackson turned his attention back to the sound and realised that a gentle chill was seeping under the foyer doors into the auditorium. The front doors of the theatre must be open. His heart started to beat faster. The darkness suddenly felt a little more unfriendly. The dragging sound continued and then the sound of someone clearing their throat, "Ahem!"

As Jackson reached the doors, the Prince huddled next to him fearfully. Needing a hand free to open the door, he reluctantly passed the crown to his companion, who immediately placed it on his head. As he did so, his elbow knocked Jackson and the sword in Jackson's hand tapped the door ever so lightly. So lightly that he hardly noticed he had done it but heavily enough for the sound to carry in the silence of the night. The sound on the other side of the doors stopped immediately and Jackson heard footsteps scuttling away. He swung the door dramatically open and the Prince gasped as they tumbled into the foyer.

The entrance doors to the Merry Theatre were thrown wide open and the light from the street lamps streamed in. The cold night air swirled around them and made Jackson shiver. He ran to the doors and out onto the pavement to check the road. Whoever had been in the foyer moments ago had escaped into the night. He turned back into the lobby, his heart racing. And then he realised, the table that the ushers used to sell programmes and ice cream from had been pushed over to the wall. Programmes were scattered all over the floor and the carpet where the table had been dragged was ripped and torn. As Jackson looked up, he saw a huge empty space where a portrait of his great-grandparents had adorned the wall for as long as he had known. Someone must have used the table to stand on to be able to steal the painting. Jackson ran back outside and looked around. The night sky was getting lighter as dawn approached. It was no use, the thief had disappeared. The Prince was looking worried as Jackson tried to close the doors. The lock had been damaged by whoever had broken in. Jackson had read about things like this in books and carried a chair across, leaning it against the door to jam it shut.

"Who would want to steal a painting?" the Prince asked, clearly confused.

"I know who it was," Jackson said, deep in thought, picturing the Weasel across the road.

"Well, if it turns out anyone needs rescuing, I'm your man!" the Prince said valiantly.

"So you won't chase me round the theatre anymore?" Jackson raised his eyebrow and the Prince smiled. They both knew they were becoming friends.

Jackson needed to tell his Mum and Dad about the break in and he needed to tell them now. He hurriedly led the Prince back to the prop store, talking continually, telling him all about what had been happening and how the theatre was under threat. What if the thief came back? What else were they planning to take and break? Luckily the Prince was surprisingly easy to coax back into the Merry Players' treasure chest. He happily swapped his crown for the promise of regaining his sword. Jackson quickly placed the crown back in the box and 'TING!' he was gone. Only then did it occur to him that he had left the Fairy Godmother by herself with the wand so he was relieved to see that is was amongst the jumble of objects. He had no idea how he was going to explain to his parents what he had been doing in the theatre in the middle of the night. He wasn't ready to tell them about the props and his Mum and Dad wouldn't believe him anyway. It was a ridiculous idea that a crown would summon a Prince and a lamp would summon a Genie, or at least the children who had played them on the stage. And that they knew his great-grandparents. How was that even possible? With his love of reading Jackson was the first person to believe in make-believe but even he struggled to make sense of it. But what did it matter how his new friends were appearing to him? The Prince had offered to help him in any way he could and the Genie and Fairy Godmother were desperate to make his wishes come true, even if they couldn't perform actual magic, and Puck was playful and ready for an adventure. Jackson had a very strong feeling that this motley mixture of well-meaning new friends would be able to help in some way. He just wasn't sure how.

CHAPTER ELEVEN

Back in the house, Jackson checked the time. It was almost two o'clock in the morning and he could hear the grumble of his Dad's snores through the floor. He ran up the stairs, with no concern for keeping quiet and knocked loudly on his parents' bedroom door.

"Jackson?" he heard his Mum say sleepily. He opened the door and let the light of the hallway shine in across the quilted bed cover. His Dad stirred.

"Mum! Dad! Someone's broken into the theatre!" Jackson blurted out.

"What?" Martha was already half out of bed and putting on her woollen dressing gown and slippers. "Albert! Someone's broken in!"

Albert was rubbing his eyes, trying to wake up. "Broken in?" he asked in a croaky voice, suddenly much more awake as Martha handed him his dressing gown to put on over his pyjamas.

"How do you know, Jackson?" Martha put her arm around her son's shoulders and was looking at him with grave concern.

"I was in there," he replied nervously.

If Albert hadn't been awake before, now he really was. "What? Why? Are you ok? Is someone in there now?"

Jackson was trying to think quickly under the scrutiny of his parents' questions. "No, they've gone. They came in the front entrance. They've taken Billy and Constance's portrait. We need to call the police."

Albert was starting to bound down the stairs. "You two stay here, I'm going to see what's going on."

"You're not going on your own, Albert!" Martha protested.

"I'll be ok. You look after Jackson," Albert called back. Jackson could hear him rustling around trying to find the stage door keys and realised he still had them in his hand. He ran down the stairs to give them to his Dad as his Mum followed hurriedly, pulling her gown around her and tying the belt.

"Why you were in the theatre at this time of night is another question all together," Albert said firmly as he opened the front door. "We'll discuss that later."

Once Albert had seen the sorry state of his usually very Merry foyer with its ripped carpet, he made his way back into the house with a heavy heart. Jackson stood in the lounge doorway watching his Dad as he picked up the telephone receiver in the hallway and dialled the number, nibbling at his fingernails nervously. Jackson could hear the mumbles of a gruff sounding policeman at the other end of the line as he took down some details and said he would be there straight away. True to his word, not fifteen minutes later Sergeant Goodman was outside the front entrance of the theatre as Albert removed the chair that was jamming the doors shut and let him in. Jackson stood back, his face feeling hot as he watched his Mum and Dad greet the policeman. Sergeant Goodman was exactly that, a good man with bushy eyebrows, ruddy cheeks and an enquiring mind. Albert knew him well as he often enjoyed performances at the Merry Theatre with his glamorous wife, Glenda. He stood strong and serious at the door as the ominous building opposite stood in darkness, the tarpaulin flapping in the breeze. The police officer inspected the damage and scribbled notes in his little black notebook.

"I know a handyman who I can send round to sort this out for you. Bob Baker. See, it just needs a bit of sanding, a lick of paint and a new lock," Sergeant Goodman smiled kindly.

"Thank you," Albert tried to smile but Jackson could see the colour draining from his face.

"And what alerted you to the break-in, Mr Merry?" the policeman asked, running his hand along the edge of the door and its broken lock as he spoke.

"My son," Albert said honestly, glancing towards Jackson.

"Well, I had better have a chat with this son of yours then," he said with a warm smile. "Shall we sit ourselves down?"

Martha placed a hand on Jackson's shoulder to reassure him. Jackson felt himself gulp, his mind was still racing, trying to think of an explanation for why he had been in the theatre in the first place. His Dad and Sergeant Goodman jammed the door shut again and they all made their way through the theatre to the house.

Jackson and his Mum sat on the sofa with mugs of hot chocolate and a blanket across their knees while his Dad and Sergeant Goodman sat in the armchairs, holding cups of tea and staring directly across at them.

"Right, young man," the policeman said addressing Jackson, "Now, I need to hear everything you can tell me about the robbery. However small and seemingly insignificant, try to tell me everything you can remember. Now let's start with *why* you were in the theatre?"

Jackson sat up straight and suddenly felt like he was in a story from one of his books. Sergeant Goodman's knees creaked as he shifted in his chair and looked across at Jackson with one bushy eyebrow raised like a runaway caterpillar on his forehead.

"I just… Well, I just wanted to practice a bit… You know, being on stage…" Well, it was half true he reasoned.

"Really?" his Dad interrupted, his eyes suddenly sparkling. His Mum signalled with her eyes that he should let his son continue.

"… but I wanted to try with no-one around… So I *borrowed* Dad's keys. And I let myself in."

Jackson gave a cautiously worded account of standing on stage, leaving out the unnecessary details and being careful not to mention his new Fairy Godmother friend and the energetic chase he had had with the Prince around the auditorium. He simply spoke of the noise that he had heard. And as notes were scribbled, Jackson finished his story, exclaiming, "It must have been that weaselly man from across the road! I know he vandalised the doors and stole the sign. And Mr Greengold must have something to do with it too!"

Martha looked worriedly at her son as the police officer responded.

"Mr Greengold?" Sergeant Goodman leant in curiously.

"He's our accountant," Albert explained and looked directly at his son. "Why would you think that?"

"He wants us to sell the theatre. He wants us to leave," Jackson stated.

His Dad stuttered, "No, no, he wants to help us Jackson. He's on our side."

76

"Then what about the man across the road?" He was exasperated now. "He knows you, Dad."

"Jackson, *everyone* in the town knows us because of the theatre."

Jackson glared at his Dad and fell silent. Sergeant Goodman, seeing his crestfallen expression, smiled kindly, "Look my lad, if you remember anything else, I want to know about it straight away! You are our key witness!"

Sergeant Goodman levered himself up from the chair and reached to shake both Martha and Albert's hands. Jackson felt the weight of the policeman's hand on his shoulder and kept his gaze on the man's shoes.

"I'll conduct some door to door enquiries and I'll send Bob round to fix your door this morning. I'll see if I can persuade him to do me a favour. He's a good man too!" he laughed a little at his own joke and Albert tried to raise a smile as he showed him to the door.

CHAPTER TWELVE

Jackson had been sent back to bed by his Mum after Sergeant Goodman had left. He crawled under the covers gratefully and fell into a deep dream-filled sleep. Dreams where Mr Green-gold, the string-haired man and the Weasel were watching him as he tried to say his line on stage, laughing at him and booing. The Fairy Godmother stood on the stage next to him waving her wand and the Genie whooshed and swooshed his arms around but nothing happened and the three men just cackled more and more loudly as the walls of the theatre started to crumble around them and the Prince and Puck chased each other round and round and round. The whole scene made Jackson feel dizzy and sick and scared. But then he stepped forward on the stage and started to speak and to his surprise, there was a hush and an audience full of familiar faces looked up at him in awe.

He woke up with a start, not knowing what he was about to say, breathing quickly and looked around his room. The books that he had planned to sell were still stacked in the cardboard box and he didn't like how the empty shelves made it look like he was moving house. He climbed out of bed sleepily and put them back in place. He wasn't moving anywhere. He needed another way to make money and his dream had given him an idea. If his Mum and Dad couldn't afford to put on another show, he would. He didn't need money, he just needed some actors. And he knew exactly where to find them.

The Weasel watched from afar as Sergeant Goodman's friendly handyman, Bob Baker, assessed the damage to the Merry Theatre's door. He watched as Albert nodded solemnly and shook the man's hand. Then, as soon as Albert had disappeared back inside, the Weasel stepped into the street and sidled towards his prey. His slicked back hair hidden under a tweed cap and his slick suit replaced with a pair of dusty overalls. He tapped his pocket to double check the replacement lock was where he had put it. A fake moustache bristled under his snouty nose and thick-framed glasses framed his weasely eyes. He cleared his throat and leant in towards his unsuspecting victim, digging his spindly fingers into his arm and speaking in a low growl.

"Don't ask any questions. Your services are no longer required. Just turn and walk away. If you don't walk now, I have ways to make you. Tell a single soul about this and you'll regret it."

Bob gulped. "Right, ok, right," he stuttered as he lowered himself down to pick up his toolbox barely daring to look around.

"Leave the tools," the Weasel said slowly and menacingly. "There's a good man."

He released his grip on Bob's arm and his victim scurried away, tripping over his own feet as he dared to glance back only once before he broke into a run. The Weasel worked quickly, using Bob's tools to fit the lock from his pocket and then testing the key before putting it in the pocket of his overalls. Perfect. No more breaking in, he would have access to the Merry Theatre whenever he wanted. He waited for Albert to return so that he could put the second part of his plan in place. He didn't have to wait long as Albert reappeared a moment later, carrying a rolled up rug. Martha was carrying the other end and the Weasel saw his opportunity.

"Let me help you with that!" he said as he rushed over and took Martha's place.

"Oh, thank you," she responded before she could realise what was happening.

Albert was concentrating on getting the rug in the right position to cover the ripped carpet and it was only when he had straightened it and looked up that he realised that the voice he had heard did not belong to Bob Baker. The Weasel smiled when he saw Albert's somewhat bemused expression.

"The boss got called away to another job. I'm standing in for now." He held his boney hand out, "Wilf," he said by way of introduction, quickly thinking of a new name for himself. Albert shook his hand, feeling uneasy but dismissing it as he had been feeling uneasy for a few days now.

"Albert," Albert said. "And this is my wife, Martha." The Weasel shook her hand too and made an effort to smile as warmly as he could, which wasn't very warmly at all. Martha smiled back.

"The lock's all fitted. Here's your new key. Keep it safe. Don't want those scoundrels coming back."

"Thanks," Albert took the new key and put it in his pocket. "Actually, would you mind having a look at some of the other repairs that we need doing? I could do with a quote."

This was going to be easier than even he had anticipated, the

Weasel thought. He closed the door and the lock secured shut with a heavy clunk, bolting them all inside. He turned, "How can I help?"

Albert led the way into the auditorium. It looked even more sorry for itself in the full glare of the house lights.

"I think painting is the first priority. The chandelier needs to be taken down and cleaned. We could really do with the carpet being replaced. And most of the seats need to be re-covered. Then backstage, we need some lighting replaced in the corridors. It would just be good to really know how much this might all cost."

The Weasel took great interest in every detail of his surroundings as they walked towards the stage. An interest that he could see Albert and Martha were mistaking for genuine concern. He really was a better actor than he gave himself credit for. Better than some of the idiots Albert had in his shows, he thought arrogantly.

"I'll put a full quote together for you. If I could just take a look at the lighting?" he asked.

As they walked up on to the stage, the sound of a telephone ringing in the office drifted through from the wings.

"I'll get it," Martha offered, heading off in the direction of the sound, only to return a couple of moments later.

"It's Mr Greengold, he's offering to introduce you to this potential buyer of his," she said to Albert and then glanced at the Weasel just in time to see a flicker of intrigue in his eyes. He could see that she realised she should not have been quite so open in front of a stranger. But it was too late and Martha had no idea of the consequences of giving away this seemingly tiny piece of information. Mr Greengold, the Weasel repeated to himself silently committing the name to memory.

Mr Greengold. He wanted to find out more about this *potential buyer*. Albert excused himself and disappeared to take the call while Martha continued leading the way backstage and the Weasel continued to play his handyman character, feigning interest in the required repairs. He'd been front of house many times before but never backstage. He noticed the wardrobe room with its rails of elaborate costumes and the prop store full of treasures and the dressing rooms full of fake jewels and discarded scripts. He noticed the drapes that shielded the wings and the ancient levers and switches that controlled the lighting. And then he noticed the ropes. The ropes that held the scenery so precariously in position and his eyes lit up with the ease of it all.

Jackson was walking across the cobbles to the stage door as Albert was seeing the Weasel out. Jackson only saw the back of the man's overalls as he disappeared around the corner of the building carrying the handyman's toolbox as if it was his own. Something about the man's walk reminded him of someone. His Mum was heading out at the same time with some posters tucked under her arm. She explained that she was meeting Stanley to put them up on every lamp post and in every shop window around town to try to sell some tickets. Jackson followed his Dad back into the theatre.

"Who was that man?" he asked with a niggling feeling at the back of his mind.

"Wilf. He's a handyman, helping us out with some repairs." Jackson had more questions but his Dad continued. "Want to help me have a bit of a clear out?"

By now they had reached the wardrobe room and Albert was looking in through the door at the rails of dresses, jackets, capes and assorted paraphernalia.

"I'm going to have a second hand sale. It'll be a good way to get rid of all the old costumes and props and make at least a few pennies to go towards renovations."

"Props?" Jackson asked, trying to hide his alarm.

His Dad was already rifling through the rail, assessing what could be sold. "Yes, we've got so many great bits and bobs. I'm sure a lot of our regulars will love the chance to buy a few bits of memorabilia. Some of these clothes could be worn out and about."

Albert was putting on a gold embroidered jacket with epaulets and fringing along the sleeves. Jackson eyed his father, his mind racing. His Dad was posing in the mirror, looking as if he was thinking of days gone by. But all Jackson could think was, did that mean *his* props too?

"But don't you need some of the props for the next show?" Jackson said nervously, trying to think of a reason for his Dad to keep hold of them.

Albert stopped for a moment, relaxing his pose so that he was suddenly simply a man in a silly outfit. "Well…" he said slowly, as though he didn't want to say what he was about to say. "We can't afford to do another show until we make some more money so we really have no choice. We're not playing games here, Jackson."

Jackson watched as his Dad took off the jacket and started to fling costumes from the rail into a pile. He had to go and hide the treasure chest. Immediately!

CHAPTER THIRTEEN

As Albert was working his way through the wardrobe room, making a pile of clothes as high as himself, Jackson was wondering how he could extract the props box. He decided he would just have to sneak it out now while his Dad wasn't looking. He let himself into the prop store quietly. A slice of light cut through the room from the window and dust sparkled across it. It seemed strange to Jackson now that there was such life in the box. The daylight made it seem like a dream. He pushed the sheets back, creating yet more dust and lifted the box up. He daren't open it now, did he? Jackson lifted the lid just to take a peek. There they were, the props. The crown, lamp, wand, flower and what was that at the bottom, glinting in the light? He put his hand in the box to push the wand to one side and to take a better look, being careful not to let any of the items tip over the edge. He hadn't seen it before, a gold ring with a single shining ruby. He was about to pick it up and then remembered. Not now! He closed the lid with a bang. As he did so, he realised his Dad was at the door.

"Ah, there you are," he seemed anxious. "Are you getting started in here?" he asked as he looked around the room thinking about what could be sold.

"Um, yes," Jackson fibbed, clinging on to the box. "Actually, I was wondering if I could have this box? I saw it the other day and I really like it. I thought I could put some of my books in it."

"Oh, that's the box I was talking about!" his Dad exclaimed. "The Merry Players box. Yes, we definitely can't sell that!" He reached forwards and took it from Jackson who had no choice but to let it go. Albert held the box with outstretched arms and studied the outside fondly. Then Jackson watched as his Dad lifted the lid and peered inside. Everything was happening in slow motion. His Dad reached his hand in. Which prop would he pull out?

"Oh yes, here's the lamp I was talking about!" Albert exclaimed, lifting it out of the box.

The Genie suddenly appeared behind him wearing a surprised expression and starting to dust himself down. Then 'TING!' he was gone as Albert placed the lamp back in the box.

"Ha!" said Jackson despite himself and his Dad mistook this for delight so continued delving around.

"Oh and I remember this ring," Albert smiled. He had the ring on the end of his first finger and was looking at it thoughtfully. Suddenly a young girl appeared from behind him, she was about Jackson's age and was wearing a simple light blue dress. Jackson thought quickly as Albert looked round at the girl with surprise.

"Can I see that?" he asked, practically snatching the ring from his Dad's hand. He couldn't let the girl disappear in front of him or he would know the secrets of the box and Jackson wasn't ready for that. He had an idea and he needed to talk to his friends about it before he told his Dad.

"Hello?" Albert said to the girl quizzically.

Jackson thought quickly, "Oh, I didn't hear you come in."

He stared at the girl willing her to magically understand but she just looked at him with a mixture of confusion and fear. "Dad, this is… Emily, my friend from… school. Mum said she could come round, we've got a holiday project." He nodded enthusiastically at the girl hoping she would go along with his story. "Mum must have left the stage door open."

"Well, hello Emily," Albert said with his mind elsewhere. "Nice to meet you. I'd better go and check that door." The girl didn't say a word but managed a smile as Albert passed the treasure chest to Jackson and left the room.

"Thank you," Jackson said, letting out a sigh of relief as soon as his Dad had gone.

"That's ok," said the girl and then added, "What for?"

"Pretending you're my imaginary friend, Emily!" Jackson laughed.

"But I'm dressed as Beauty."

"From Beauty and the Beast!" Jackson exclaimed with a look of realisation.

The girl nodded. "That's my ring isn't it?" she asked looking at Jackson's hand. He allowed her to take it and she slipped it onto her finger. She admired it as it sparkled in the light. "It's meant to take me back to the Beast's castle when I put it on. But it's only a prop really."

"It's much more than a prop!" Jackson exclaimed. "It's magic! It makes you appear when I take it out of this box and then disappear again when I put it back in. Like the others."

"The others told me about you. I can't believe it happened to me too! They're all desperate to come back to see you."

"Really! That's brilliant because I'm desperate to see them too. I really need you all to help me. But first, let's get out of here. I can't risk my Mum and Dad seeing all of you."

Now that his Dad had seen Beauty once, Jackson walked boldly down the corridor with her. Albert was distracted, checking if the stage door lock was working properly after 'Emily' had been able to get in so easily. He wasn't listening as his son explained that they were going back to the house to get started on their school project. A project that wasn't for school at all. A project that Jackson had named, 'Saving The Merry Theatre'.

Beauty followed Jackson into the house looking around with great curiosity. She twirled the ring, spinning it round and round her finger as they climbed the stairs. Jackson was taking two steps at a time, bounding towards his room, holding the Merry Players' box out in front of him. When they got inside, he turned to Beauty, "Close the door, quick!"

Beauty did so and Jackson tipped the box up and emptied its contents on to his bedspread. Out tumbled the wand, the crown, the lamp and the flower and there was a hustle and bustle as the characters sprang out of thin air. The Prince brandishing his sword ready for action, the Genie poised to throw confetti, the Fairy Godmother straightening her wig and Puck jumping straight up on to the bed and looking ready for mischief. It took them all a second to realise they were in a bedroom instead of the theatre and another moment to realise that they were all looking at each other. Excited butterflies fluttered in Jackson's stomach.

"Welcome to the first meeting of the new, well, not new, but newly reformed Merry Players!" he announced. There was much chattering and giggling. The Prince was saying hello to the Fairy Godmother and Beauty so they clearly knew each other from their parts in plays directed by Jackson's great-grandmother. And Puck had jumped down from the bed and was hugging the Genie who then turned to Jackson.

"Did the theatre get saved then? Are we celebrating?" the Genie asked eagerly, remembering his last meeting with Jackson and how he had so desperately wanted his wish to come true.

"Not quite. Not yet. That's why I need you all to help me. If you want to?"

The Fairy Godmother stepped forward. "Of course, we'll help you."

The Prince then said valiantly, "If the theatre's in trouble then the Merry Players are in trouble too. We'll do whatever it takes."

Puck grinned mischievously and repeated, "Whatever it takes!"

"Why does the theatre need saving?" Beauty asked.

Jackson sat down on the bed, ready to explain. Puck jumped down and sat cross-legged on the floor ready to hear Jackson's story. He explained about the money problems and how he had wanted to sell his books to help and how his Dad was now selling as many costumes and props as he could to make money. He told them about the state the theatre was in, how they had found the vandalised posters and how he had witnessed the break-in. How the Merry Theatre sign and his great-grandparents' portrait had both been stolen. He told them that he didn't trust Mr Greengold one little bit since he had mentioned selling the theatre. And then described the measly weaselly Weasel across the road and the puffed-up angry string-haired man who seemed to own the building and how they had said they knew his Dad. And how he had seen Harry going inside and how he just *knew* they were all hiding something.

And he finished by explaining that his Mum and Dad were so broke that they couldn't even afford to put on their next show.

"And so that is what we are going to do. We are going to be the next show!"

The Merry Players looked at Jackson with mixed expressions. The Genie, the real showman in the room, was the first to speak. "Brilliant! What show are we doing?"

Jackson, who hadn't quite thought that far ahead in his plan tried to think of an answer, "Well, I haven't got to that bit yet. I was hoping that you might have some ideas."

Puck jumped up, "How about…" she paused dramatically, "A Midsummer Night's Dream? It's poetic and dramatic and magical and ex…"

"Or!" the Genie interrupted, "Aladdin! A mysterious tale of adventure in a mystical land." He put his hand out in front of him and looked along his arm, looking far into the distance.

"Or!" the Prince stepped forward with his suggestion. "Cinderella! It's classic and dramatic and there's a GREAT ball!" With that he took the Fairy Godmother's hand and span her round. She giggled and finished her spin facing Jackson, "And I get to grant wishes!"

"I can grant wishes too!" the Genie chipped in.

"And I can make *magic* happen!" Puck exclaimed.

Beauty finally spoke up, "But Beauty and the Beast has the romance of Cinderella *and* the magic of all of your stories."

Jackson listened to all of their pleas. "How do we choose?"

Just as he asked the question, he heard the front door open and his Mum's voice calling up the stairs, "Jackson!"

He gasped. "Ssshhhhh!" he whispered urgently to the group and they all fell silent, apart from Puck who repeated, "Ssshhhhh!" and Jackson glared at her. He could hear his

Mum's footsteps on the stairs. He started grabbing the props and throwing them back into the box.

"Sorry!" he whispered to everyone and no one at the same time and four of them vanished. Beauty remained, her eyes wide with shock as her friends disappeared around her.

"Just go along with what I say!" Jackson pleaded.

The door opened and he shuffled over to obscure the box. His Mum looked in with a smile on her face, "That's all the posters out. They're all over town! We should get some tickets sold." Then seeing Beauty, "Oh hello?"

"Hi," said Beauty.

"Um… Beaut… I mean, Emily's come round to work on our school project together," Jackson rambled.

"Great! Nice to meet you Emily. I'm Martha, Jackson's mum." And she looked at Beauty and then at Jackson, knowing the way that only mothers do that something wasn't quite right.

"Looks like you need some drinks and snacks. I'll pop and get you some biscuits." She smiled and left the room, padding back down the stairs and leaving Jackson and Beauty wondering what to do next.

It didn't feel safe to get the other props back out with his Mum in the house. Beauty turned to look along Jackson's bookshelves, brushing her hand along the titles and stopping occasionally to pull a book out to look at the cover.

"So what can we do for our show? Everyone wants something different," Jackson frowned.

"Have you read ALL of these?" she asked in amazement. Jackson nodded coyly and a look of inspiration spread across Beauty's face, "You must know so many stories! Why don't we make something up?"

Jackson thought for a moment and stood up to join her at the shelves. He looked along the spines at the exciting titles. Thick and thin books full of adventures. "I like that idea. We could have all of you in one show. We'll make a story up that gives you all a starring role."

"Brilliant!" Beauty grinned as Jackson looked around to find some paper and pencils. Now it really did look like they were doing a school project as they sat on the floor scribbling.

"You and the Prince could be a King and Queen! He likes wearing his crown so he'd like that. And you live in a beautiful castle," Jackson began.

"I like the sound of that," Beauty smiled, writing notes on her paper.

"And Puck's mischievous so I think she'd quite like playing the baddie," Jackson spoke quickly now. The ideas had started to flow and he couldn't get his words out fast enough. "And she could cast a spell on you!"

"What kind of spell?" Beauty asked. They thought for a moment.

"One that makes the castle become dark and scary. One where everything slowly starts to fall apart..."

At that moment, his Mum appeared at the door with a tray of blackcurrant cordial and ginger biscuits for them to share. Jackson and Beauty tucked in eagerly and as his Mum left the room, Jackson noticed the sad look on her face. If his parents had lost hope, the Merry Players would be the ones to bring it back. This play was going to fix it all. It was going to be brilliant. And not only was it going to be brilliant. It was going to save the Merry Theatre.

CHAPTER FOURTEEN

The following morning, the Weasel was ready to set about the next part of his plan. He pressed his fake moustache firmly to his upper lip, put on the thick-framed glasses and pulled the flat cap on to his head, glancing at himself in the mirror as he left. In his handyman disguise, he found himself missing the need to sneak around corners as he walked boldly up to the front door of the Merry Theatre in broad daylight. Martha was holding a broom as she opened the door.

"Mrs Merry," the Weasel mumbled.

"Ah, Wilf! I wondered when you'd be coming back in to see us. Have you got that quote ready?" Martha asked.

"Just need a couple more measurements to make sure all the calculations are correct." The Weasel pulled a measuring tape from the inside pocket of his overalls and Martha nodded as the pair walked down the side of the auditorium together.

"Albert's backstage," Martha said softly by way of explanation. "We're just checking some electrics so excuse the lights going on and off. Seems we've got some issues there too," she explained with a sigh as they reached the wing and lights flickered on and off in various combinations on the stage. "George, this is our handyman, Wilf."

George was staring intently at a panel of switches. "Hello

there," he said barely looking up.

"Well, carry on! You know where everything is!" Martha smiled warmly and left the Weasel in the wing. He shuffled around for a moment, feigning interest in his surroundings. Really he was quietly checking that he could still carry out his plan with George being so close by. He thought quickly and stepped out onto the edge of the stage, coughing heavily as he did so. George looked round, distracted.

"Oh, I am sorry to interrupt you," the Weasel smiled. "It's just I noticed the spotlight on the left looks a little dull." George looked at the Weasel a little confused as he continued, "You'll know better than me. Take a look."

George shrugged and turned to shuffle past, onto the stage. It was even easier than the Weasel could imagine. But with George only distracted briefly, he had to act quickly. Stepping behind the set, he pulled a knife out of his pocket and grabbed the rope that held the scenery in place, noticing it was already worn. Perfect. Nobody would suspect a thing. No reason to believe that the innocent handyman Wilf was involved. He could hear Albert whistling to himself somewhere on the other side of the scenery. What did he have to be so cheery about? It made the Weasel even more determined. He held the knife against the rope. Gently does it. Just a few frayed pieces, enough to make it weak. The threads of the rope gave way, untwisting, becoming looser. And looser.

Just in time too, the Weasel thought, as George came back into the wing.

"Doesn't look dull to me. I'll test some more combinations," George muttered and shuffled back to the lighting panel.

"Must be my eyes," the Weasel said slowly with a sinister

smile. But George wasn't looking. A man of few words, he was already busy flicking switches again.

"How are we doing?" came a voice from the other side of the drape. It was Albert. Perfect timing, the Weasel thought as he stepped onto the edge of the stage, ensuring he kept out of the shadow of the scenery. He wasn't stupid.

"All done, Mr Merry. I'll bring the quote round in the next day or two. Definitely a few more repairs to do back here," the Weasel stated, forcing a grimace, feeling queasy at having to appear friendly.

"Thanks Wilf, let's go through them once your quote is ready. I'll have to thank the Sergeant for putting us in touch. I'm really grateful for your help."

The Weasel raised an eyebrow. He knew the moment Albert had that conversation, his cover would be blown. "Oh don't bother Sergeant Goodman. It's my pleasure. I'll see myself out."

"Thank you, Wilf." As Albert smiled, the Weasel was gone, with a deep sense of satisfaction at the thought of what he'd just done and what was about to happen. Albert walked purposefully over to the lighting panel, "Ok George, let's have another look at these spotlights."

The crash was so loud and the scream so piercing that Jackson could hear them in the house. He leapt up from the floor of his bedroom where he was sitting with Beauty working on their play. He had been careful to only summon her from the props box that morning as he needed some time to quietly contemplate the ideas they had started working on the day before.

Beauty's eyes widened with alarm, "What was that?"

94

"I'd better go and see," Jackson said. "Sorry, I'll bring you back later, I promise!"

Beauty nodded her head, letting Jackson know she was ready. He dropped the ring back in the box and in an instant, she was gone, back to his great-grandmother. Jackson pushed the wooden chest right under his bed, pulling the bedspread down to cover the gap between the bed and the floor. He scrambled back to his feet and ran towards the sound, taking the stairs two at a time.

Once inside the theatre he could hear his Mum repeating, "Oh my goodness! Oh my goodness! George! Say something!"

As Jackson rounded the corner into the wing, he saw George lying on the floor, motionless. He stopped. His Mum was kneeling over George, her expression full of fear. She spotted him.

"Jackson! Pass me the cushion from that chair, quickly!" The set had fallen heavily on George's leg and Albert was attempting to pull the heavy wooden board up so that it wasn't resting on him. Jackson handed the cushion to his Mum and then attempted to help his Dad with the weight of the set.

"We've never had any trouble with the ropes before. I barely touched it," Albert rambled, tears welling in his eyes. Jackson had seen his Dad cry with happiness before, touched by the line in a play or the curtain call but he realised he had never seen him cry tears of upset before.

Suddenly, there was a gentle murmur. "What happened?"

"Oh, George! Are you ok?" Albert exclaimed, heavy tears now falling from his eyes onto the floorboards.

"Give him a minute, Albert, he's only just come to!" Martha said sharply. Jackson looked from his Mum to his Dad anxiously and then stepped forwards. "George, it's ok. You'll be ok."

"What happened?" George muttered again.

"The set fell. Can you open your eyes? Can you see me?" Martha said in a soothing voice.

George squinted at her, trying to lift his head. "Doris, is that you?"

Martha looked up at Albert, concerned and slid the cushion under George's head as he closed his eyes again.

Suddenly, there was another voice. Seamus appeared next to Jackson. "What on earth...?" Seamus trailed off in shock at the scene before him.

"I don't understand it. I barely touched it. It just... fell," Albert said in disbelief as Seamus rushed over to him. Quickly assessing the situation, Seamus ushered Jackson to one side and took some of the weight of the set from his boss. He was clearly the stronger of the two men but even he seemed to be straining under the weight. The three of them pushed and scraped the set heavily across the stage until they were able to lower it away from George.

"I'll call the doctor," Martha announced, getting to her feet. Albert watched her as she walked into the wing. Jackson could see how shaken he was.

Doctor Edwards arrived quickly. Having been a friend of the Merrys for some years, he was shocked to receive Martha's call and had rushed to attend to George immediately. With his glasses perched on the end of his nose, he announced that he suspected heavy bruising and concussion rather than any broken limbs.

"I would advise a night or two in hospital anyway. I'd like

to keep an eye on him. Now, can you tell me what happened, George?"

George's voice was shaky, "I was just walking out onto the stage to check one of the spotlights and I realised the set seemed to be moving. I thought maybe I was just tired. And then, well, it happened very quickly, suddenly, it fell and I didn't have time to get fully out of the way." He winced and clenched his jaw in pain.

Doctor Edwards scribbled. Jackson kept quiet but his mind was racing. Why was his Dad staying silent? How had the set just fallen like that?

Jackson watched as his Dad and Seamus lifted the set back into place, securing it with new ropes. He also watched as his Dad studied the old frayed rope curiously before coiling it up and carrying it down the corridor to the office.

CHAPTER FIFTEEN

Jackson reached under his bed and slid the treasure chest out, flinging the top open and tipping the props out onto the floor. Ting! Ting! Ting! Ting! Ting! His newfound friends appeared at once. It was rather crowded in Jackson's tiny bedroom but they crammed in, waiting excitedly for him to speak. Jackson began to tell the story that he and Beauty had started to write.

"So Prince, you and Beauty will be the King and Queen..."

"So I'm in it from the beginning?" the Prince asked. "I'm usually the one who comes in to save the day..."

"Well, yes, but... Let me just tell you what happens first," Jackson said, trying to be patient. The Prince raised an eyebrow, which Jackson chose to ignore. "So you are the King and Queen, living happily in a beautiful castle but you don't have any children."

"I could be their child!" Puck piped up.

"Yes, you could be but you're not," Beauty stated bluntly, hoping she was helping Jackson but only succeeding in making the usually spritely Puck look a little put out. "Jackson will tell us..."

"I could grant a wish to give them a child!" the Genie interrupted. "I'd be amazing at that."

"You could and you would be, but you arrive later. Puck is

the one who will cast the first spell," Beauty said firmly. "Let Jackson tell you!"

"But Puck doesn't cast spells, she tricks people," the Genie complained. "I'm the one who grants wishes."

"Well, I do that too," the Fairy Godmother chipped in, picking up her wand and waving it around.

"With a single call, I will trick you all!" said Puck, springing up onto the bed dramatically.

Jackson took a breath. "BUBBLEPUMPKIN!" he shouted suddenly. And everyone stopped and looked at him bemused and amused. A smile spread across the Fairy Godmother's face as she realised that Jackson had plucked up his courage to be centre of attention. Jackson's face flushed red as he wavered for a moment. He knew they were all now waiting for him to speak.

"I would like to direct the play," he finally said, his voice wobbling. "And *I* would like to tell you what happens."

To his surprise, there was a chorus of approval. He felt his confidence grow a little. The piece of paper that he and Beauty had been scribbling on earlier was folded in his pocket and he now spread it out on the floor, ironing out the creases with his hands. They all knelt down around the page and listened to Jackson attentively.

"Now. Puck, you were once a magical, kind sprite but you were tricked by an evil spirit who cast you out of the village and doomed you to bring misery to all who cross your path. You know the King and Queen long for a child so you leave an orphaned baby by their door. They have no idea where the baby came from but they see her as a great gift. But what they don't know is that she brings a curse with her that will rob them of all their riches and will take all of the light out of their lives."

"Wow!" Puck stared, open-mouthed. "It sounds like a big part!" She grinned happily at the character she had been given to play.

"So the child grows up. Fairy Godmother, I'd like you to play her," Jackson said looking at his friend. "It's a very important role," he added with a smile.

The Fairy Godmother looked at him with tears of joy springing to her eyes. "Really? Goodness. Thank you, Jackson. I'll work really hard. And I'll make you really proud."

Jackson grinned, then glanced across at the Prince, who looked a little put out. "So, I need you to be a really strong King. Your castle is going to start crumbling around you. Just like the theatre is crumbling around us…" He looked thoughtful for a moment and then gathered himself. "As your daughter grows, the trees lose their leaves, the plants in the garden stop flowering. The fires won't light."

"So I come to the rescue!" the Prince blurted out enthusiastically rising up on his knees and holding his arms out triumphantly.

"Not quite…" Jackson replied as the Prince sank back down. "You and the Queen are more and more mystified. You start to realise that maybe your daughter is cursed. When she tries to make a fire it goes out. When she harvests vegetables from the garden, they go rotten. Puck is determined that you will cast her out into the cold just as she was cast out and becomes more and more angry when you don't. She makes the castle completely uninhabitable. And when you still stay loyal to your daughter, Puck finally snaps and casts a spell to banish you and the Queen to the tower and makes poison ivy grow all around it so you are separated from your daughter forever."

The Prince tutted and shook his head in objection, "I wouldn't get captured. I'm *always* the hero. I would capture Puck. I would save the day."

Jackson hesitated, thinking for a moment before the Fairy Godmother piped up, surprising herself with her own authority. "This is *Jackson's* play, not yours."

"Well, I still think that…" The Prince drifted off as the Fairy Godmother glared at him. "Ok," he relented. "Then what happens?"

"The daughter is lonely in the ruined castle, listening to the cries of the King and Queen with her home falling apart around her. She knows that Puck has put a spell on her, so she needs to find a way to remove the spell."

The Fairy Godmother listened eagerly and Jackson paused for a moment, "Well, that's kind of as far as we've got…"

Jackson looked at the Genie, who had been quiet for an unusual amount of time. He had been hanging on Jackson's every word and now was his chance. The words were on the tip of his tongue and he couldn't hold it in any longer, "She could find… a lamp?"

Jackson looked at him and suddenly he felt his whole body tingle with excitement. What a brilliant idea. It was perfect. "Just like I found the lamp when everything was starting to fall apart. Just like I found you."

"Yes!" the Genie jumped up excitedly.

The Fairy Godmother was on her feet, tiptoeing around the room delicately picking her way through some imaginary undergrowth. "So, I'm in the garden, in the cold, looking around for food to eat and I see something gold sparkling in the darkness."

Jackson watched entranced as Beauty picked the lamp up

from the bed and handed it to the Fairy Godmother who held it like a precious jewel.

"And Puck appears just at that moment, furious that she's forgotten about the lamp. Furious that I've found it!" the Fairy Godmother said.

Puck jumped up. Even the Prince was enraptured now, watching the two girls as they circled each other.

"Give it to me!" Puck demanded, fully lost in her role. "Give it to me or I'll make your home and your parents disappear forever!"

Jackson gasped despite himself, "So Fairy Godmother, you don't know if Puck is capable of such a thing but you can't risk losing your home and your parents. So you slowly hand over the lamp."

"Oh. Really?" the Genie looked at Jackson, full of disappointment.

"But!" Jackson grinned. He realised he was really enjoying how his friends were on the edge of their seats, listening to his every word. "But!" he repeated. "As you hand the lamp over to Puck, you brush it past your other hand and..."

"Alacadabrazam!" the Genie suddenly shouted.

"Exactly!" Jackson exclaimed. "The Genie appears..."

"Whoosh!" The Genie blew the word through his teeth and threw out his arms.

"And he throws gold confetti into the air. And it blows around and it covers the castle and it covers the garden..." Jackson continued.

The Prince giggled and clapped his hands in delight imagining the confetti falling all around him.

Puck leapt up again, "But you will see! You will see that you can't defeat me!" she teased.

Jackson leapt up too, unable to contain his excitement as he leant into the circle and continued his story. "Ah! But there is so much gold confetti that it completely fills the air. And Puck, it also covers you."

Puck stared at Jackson, waiting for his next line.

"And as it falls onto you, the spell is broken and you transform back into a beautiful, pixie-like child. A magical, bright sprite. Which is who you have really been all along."

Puck beamed from ear to ear as Jackson continued, "And the leaves on the trees start to grow and flowers start to appear all across the garden. And the poison ivy around the tower falls to the ground and disappears..."

"... and the sun glows in the sky like a big piece of gold confetti!" the Genie added.

"Why not?" Jackson laughed.

"And I suppose the King finally arrives to save the day?" the Prince said dryly. Beauty burst into giggles and put her arm around the Prince's shoulders to give him a squeeze.

"And the King and Queen hug their daughter and the Genie and Puck dance around in the sunlight and they all live happily ever after."

"And the audience give us a standing ovation!" the Genie exclaimed starting to clap emphatically. All of the friends joined in, whooping and cheering and Jackson couldn't stop himself from taking a bow.

CHAPTER SIXTEEN

As Jackson walked back into the theatre, he could hear raised voices.

"There's no one else to do it! I can muddle through."

"Albert, I know you know the play but you don't know everything George does with those lights! It's impossible."

"I'm not cancelling the show, Martha! We're losing money as it is! We can't afford to cancel."

"Maybe I could try?" Jackson heard his Mum offer.

"Then what about the costume changes and props being ready. Louisa can't help with that, she'll be on stage."

Jackson closed the stage door quietly behind him and walked down the corridor towards his parents.

"I could do it," he interrupted.

As the words came out of his mouth, he couldn't believe what he was saying. The confidence he had just felt with his friends had obviously gone to his head.

His parents looked at him, surprised.

"Jackson, it's wonderful of you to offer but you can't do it. You're only ten. It's much too responsible a job," Martha said kindly.

"I watch the show every night and I've watched George so many times. I know every cue. He even lets me flick the switches sometimes. I know I could do it."

Albert looked at his son proudly. "Really? You know the cues?" Jackson felt like hadn't seen this look from his Dad for a long time.

"Yes, I know the whole show pretty much off by heart."

"Come and show me," his Dad said.

"Don't you think this is a lot of responsibility to give your son, Albert?" Martha asked, following them down the corridor.

"I can do it, Mum. Just give me a chance."

As they reached the lighting panel, Jackson could feel his heart beating in his chest. Why had he said he would do this? It felt like a moment of madness. Now his parents were watching him expectantly, waiting for him to prove himself. But how could he back out now? He had said he wanted to save the theatre. He had said he could do it. Now he had to prove it. George's cue sheet was next to the lighting board. On it, scribbles showing the sequence of the switches for each scene. Jackson looked at it realising he didn't really understand the instructions. He had never looked at the paperwork before, he just *knew* it.

"So, how do we open?" his Mum asked in a slightly shaky voice. His Dad looked at him in anticipation. Jackson looked at the switches and then back at the paper. The words seemed to be moving and blurry. He blinked a couple of times trying to focus and then glanced across at the stage. The same view he had night after night.

"Jackson?" his Dad said uncertainly.

As Jackson looked towards the stage, he imagined Harry stepping out into the light.

"That's right," he thought. "The whole thing is flooded with light at the opening." He turned and changed the settings. "So we open like this," he said out loud. And Albert smiled.

"Then in the next scene, it's just Seamus and Louisa talking so it changes to two spots on them, like this." Jackson could see them in his mind's eye now, lit in the middle of the stage.

On he went, scene by scene, getting into a rhythm now. His parents stood either side of him, relaxing more and more as they realised Jackson really *did* know what he was doing.

"And then they come on for their curtain call and the stage is flooded with light again," he said finally looking up.

"Well, Jackson. You've got the job!" his Dad said as he put his arm around his shoulders and gave him a squeeze.

The audience had taken their seats and as the chatter died down, Harry stepped on to the stage. Albert pulled at the ropes. The curtains opened with a heavy swoosh and Jackson took his first cue, flicking the switches confidently. His face felt hot and he was sure he could hear his pulse in his ears. He swallowed and focused intently on Harry's words. He let his fingers rest gently on the next switches and waited for the precise moment that he had seen George do this many times. With a gentle click, the lights changed so that the two spotlights shone perfectly on Seamus and Louisa as Harry left the stage and they started to speak. Jackson felt his breath settle just a little. The cues felt like a rhythm to him, etched on his memory like a song.

"Lovely work with the lights, Jackson. I'm impressed!" Harry whispered as he stood waiting for his next scene.

"Harry," Jackson whispered back, looking away from the switches. "Can I talk to you after the show?"

"Of course, what's the matter?" Harry mouthed quizzically.

Jackson glanced over Harry's shoulder to see that Seamus and Louisa were still in the middle of their scene. He looked back at Harry. "The man you met, over the road, who is he?"

It wasn't Jackson's imagination, Harry looked shocked. It seemed to take him a moment to gather himself. "Over the road? I don't know anyone over the road."

"But, I saw you..." Jackson trailed off as he realised that Seamus was repeating his line. Harry had missed his cue. And that meant that Jackson had missed the lighting cue too.

"Oh goodness!" Harry said under his breath as he quickly turned and stepped back onto the stage to confused looks from the audience.

Jackson gulped, looking frantically at the lighting board. Which switch was it? Not that one. Which one was it? Harry was out of the light and talking in semi-darkness on the stage. Quickly! Suddenly an arm appeared over his shoulder and a hand flicked the correct switch down. Jackson looked up to see his Dad looking exasperated.

"Come on, Jackson. I'll take over. You obviously can't be trusted to concentrate!"

"But I... It was only one cue..." Jackson protested quietly.

"Go and sit in the office. I'll have to do the rest of the show. Go on, let me concentrate!"

The look of pride on his Dad's face had disappeared and Jackson realised there was no point protesting. Why had he let thoughts of the Weasel distract him? He was cross with himself and stomped down the corridor towards the office, knocking Louisa's arm on the way past.

"Are you ok, Jackson?" she whispered kindly but he couldn't bring himself to reply.

Jackson really wanted to slam the door but his conscience stopped him and he closed it quietly. He didn't want to disrupt the play any more than he had done already. He slumped down in his Dad's chair and sighed, feeling defeated. He spun around, trying to distract himself. Looking down he noticed the shelves full of files bursting with paperwork. Before he knew it, he was reaching down and grabbing at the files. He scanned page after page of figures desperately trying to make sense of the scribbles. He still wanted to get to the bottom of what Mr Greengold's intentions were but all the pages proved was what he already knew. The Merry was heavily in debt and even Jackson knew the cost of all of the repairs must be astronomical compared to the theatre's earnings. As he slid the papers back into the files, something caught his eye. There, tucked in the corner of the office, was the frayed piece of rope. He walked across to it, knelt down and studied it closely. It wasn't just worn, it looked like it had been cut, with a knife. Jackson gulped and put it back exactly how he had found it.

It was time for the curtain call and Jackson leant against the wall watching as his Dad flooded the stage with light. He could hear waves of cheering and clapping as the actors took their bows. Jackson looked down at his shoes and avoided his Dad's gaze. Harry was the last to emerge, looking back across the stage. He looked almost wistful, Jackson thought as he followed him out into the corridor.

"Harry?" he called after him. Harry turned. Jackson could see it. He looked nervous.

"What is it, Jackson?"

"I know I saw you. It *was* you."

Jackson was sure that Harry almost stopped breathing.

There was a pause before he spoke, "It wasn't me."

"But I saw you shake hands with a man in a grey suit and you went inside the old town hall."

Harry hesitated, "Must have been someone else. Sorry."

He smiled awkwardly and disappeared into the dressing room leaving Jackson feeling confused. A few minutes later Harry re-emerged, now in his own clothes, the magic of his character removed.

"Can you give this to your Mum and Dad, please?" he asked Jackson with a quiver in his voice, handing a sealed brown envelope to him. "Tell them I'm sorry."

Jackson took the envelope and looked at the writing on the front, 'To Albert & Martha'. Harry reached out and ruffled Jackson's hair and while Jackson frowned, Harry walked away from him silently, pulling his collar up around his ears.

Once the last of the audience and actors had left, Jackson found his parents on the stage, rearranging the props and furniture.

"The rope was tampered with!" he blurted out, confronting his Dad more directly than he had ever dared before. "I saw it in your office. Somebody had cut it."

Albert looked as his son, taken aback. Martha frowned. Jackson wondered if he was about to shout at him that he should mind his own business. But then he simply said, "I know."

Well, Jackson hadn't expected that. "Really?"

"Of course, I saw it when we took it down. I just have no idea who on earth would want to do such a thing."

"We're just glad George is ok, that's all that matters," Jackson's Mum added.

"But what about everything else that's happened?"

"What's that?" his Dad suddenly demanded, catching sight of the envelope in his son's hand.

Jackson passed it to him, "It's from Harry. He said to tell you he was sorry. But Dad…"

Albert tore the envelope open, unfolded the letter inside and scanned it quickly, his mouth open in shock.

"Harry's handed in his notice," Albert said as he sank down to kneel on the floor, re-reading the lines on the page. "As of now."

Jackson wasn't surprised. He knew something odd was going on. He sat down on the floorboards in front of his Dad.

"I saw Harry. Outside the old town hall. He was meeting the man I saw in the theatre the other night," he said.

Albert looked up from the letter, puzzled.

"What are you saying, Jackson?" his Mum asked.

Jackson continued, "They looked like they knew each other. He denied it though. He said he wasn't there."

"That doesn't mean anything," his Dad snapped. "He doesn't say why he's leaving, just that it's with immediate effect."

"But tomorrow's the last night. Who's going to play his part in the show?"

"Good question."

Jackson jumped up. "You know the lines!"

"I do, but I haven't acted for a long time."

"You can do it, Albert," Martha said encouragingly.

Jackson thought about how he had found his courage when he had been with the Merry Players. He wanted his Dad to find that same courage, even with all the uncertainty they were facing. "You can do it, Dad. You can't just give up. You have to do it."

His Dad looked at him, deep in thought. Jackson tried to

work out what he was thinking. Was it determination? Was it defeat? Or was it guilt about what had happened to George?

CHAPTER SEVENTEEN

It was either very, very late or very, very early depending on how you looked at it. Jackson had pretended to be asleep until his parents had gone to bed but since then he had been scribbling on page after page, preparing a script for his play rehearsals. Finally he felt he had enough to work with. He crept, step by step, down the stairs, carrying the treasure chest carefully under his arm and his scribbled script folded up in his school bag slung across his shoulder. He reached up on to the shelf and felt around. The keys weren't there! Maybe his parents had hidden them after the night of the break in. He tiptoed into the kitchen. The moonlight was streaming in through the window and there, sparkling in its glow, was the new front door key. He let himself out of the house and tiptoed around the front of the building. All the while unaware that he was being watched by a weaselly figure who was hiding in the shadows of the scaffolding.

Jackson locked himself in. Coming in through the front door of the theatre made him feel even more nervous than he already was but if the Merry Players were going to put on a show they needed to rehearse. The aftermath of the break-in seemed even more sinister in the shadows so he was keen to have company. He stopped in the foyer to empty the props box, carefully putting the ring and flower in his pocket and looping the crown around his arm so that he could still hold the wand and lamp in one hand. His friends appeared immediately in the darkness, rustling and shuffling around trying to work out where they were. Jackson herded them into the auditorium as they all giggled and whispered.

"Time for rehearsals!" he announced.

He knew exactly where to find the light switches for the auditorium, behind a hidden panel by the doors. He reached in and click, click, click, the stalls were flooded with light. The players rushed towards the front and bounded up the stairs on to the stage. Jackson took a deep breath and walked towards them. He was ready to direct. Well, that's what he told himself anyway.

On the stage, Jackson put the treasure chest down, carefully placed the crown, lamp and wand beside it and checked the ring and flower were safe in his trouser pocket. He took the rolled up script from his school bag and straightened it out, clearing his throat. In the middle of the stage, the Prince appeared to be practising galloping. He came to a standstill next to Jackson.

"Have you got an actual horse for me to ride? I'll need a horse if I'm going to play a King," he stated, a little out of breath,

Jackson replied tentatively, feeling the answer was perhaps obvious but not wanting to be rude. "No, I don't have a horse."

"So, how will the audience know I'm riding one?"

"Well," Jackson thought for a moment, "It will be obvious because you'll be *galloping*."

The Prince didn't seem convinced but galloped off again nonetheless. The Genie and Fairy Godmother were having a 'wish-off'. Whooshing and swooshing their arms around and making all sorts of shusssshing and shoooooping noises. Beauty and Puck were chasing each other around in figures of eight.

"Right," said Jackson, hoping to get some attention. And then, "Right!" a little louder. The galloping and whooshing and chasing continued.

"GLITTERBOOM!" Jackson shouted and laughed at himself as everyone stopped and looked at him. He smiled, "Let's rehearse. I've written a script."

Everyone gathered around and Jackson became conscious that all eyes were on him, waiting for him to speak. "So... so," he stuttered slightly, "Puck, you're on stage first."

Puck leant in, poised for action and paying full attention.

"So," Jackson said again. "You spring into the scene, running around and weaving in and out of the trees in the garden approaching the castle."

Puck immediately ran across the stage and started springing around like an excitable frog jumping from one spot to another, "Like this?"

"Er... Yes," Jackson said, thinking 'no' but not being brave enough to say. "And you tell the audience that you were once banished from the village because an evil spirit cast a spell on you that doomed you to bring misery to everyone you meet. I'll give you some words to say."

Puck was springing back towards the group, "And where will the trees and flowers be?"

Jackson hesitated. "Um... Dotted around," he said somewhat vaguely, keeping his eyes on his script. He hadn't really thought about that yet so quickly changed the subject. "While Puck's hiding behind a tree, Beauty and Prince, you enter, walking through your garden talking about how happy you are."

Beauty listened attentively as he continued. "But you also tell the audience that you long for a child."

"I'll need a crown if I'm a Queen. Can I wear a crown?" Beauty asked.

"You could wear the Prince's crown," Jackson offered.

"No she can't, I need it to play the King!" the Prince said bluntly.

Jackson couldn't help rolling his eyes. "Ok, Beauty, you can always pretend and the audience will know because your acting will be so good."

"Oh, ok," Beauty said looking disappointed.

"And then, once you are in the castle…" Jackson changed his tone to convey the drama of the next scene. "Puck creeps in with a baby in her arms."

"Do we have a baby?" asked Puck curiously.

"Well, not an actual baby, obviously," Jackson replied, getting a little irritated by all the questions.

"Maybe a doll. Do you have a doll?" the Genie chipped in.

"Well, no… We'll pretend! You always say how the audience have to use their imagination," Jackson said, trying to be positive.

"For wishes, yes. They definitely need to use their imagination for wishes. But we usually have a set around us, like this. And we have props. Well, you know we have props." He indicated the collection of items next to the Merry Players box on the floor. "So the audience kind of have more of an idea of what's going on."

Jackson looked up at the set, suddenly feeling rather unsettled at the sight of it looming high above them.

"Yes, we usually have props," added Beauty. This brought

Jackson's attention back to her as he thought about the fact that Beauty herself was the result of a magical prop.

"We haven't got any money to make a set of a garden or a castle or to buy props," Jackson said with disappointment in his voice. "The whole reason we're doing this is to make money, not spend it."

The Fairy Godmother had been quietly listening and finally spoke. "You could be the narrator. You could set the scene for the audience." She smiled at Jackson as if she knew exactly what he was thinking. He felt the redness rising in his face again and his nerves tingling from his toes to the top of his head. The Fairy Godmother stepped forwards and put her hand on his arm.

"You could do it. You'd be brilliant," she said kindly. Jackson was silent. "I know you think it would be scary but look at what you're doing now. You're directing us and talking on stage to all of us."

Beauty joined in, "That's a great idea! You could read from a script so you wouldn't have to remember lines and you could tell everyone that there's a garden and a castle and that Puck used to be a sprite."

"And that I have a galloping horse," the Prince added, a little miserably.

Never mind the Prince, Jackson's heart was galloping as fast as a horse right now. Could he do it? Stand on the stage in front of all of those staring eyes? Making sets and props would cost money that they didn't have and take time and they didn't have that either. If there was ever a time to be brave, this was it.

"Ok! I'll do it!" The words burst out of his mouth before he could think any more. If it meant helping to save the Merry

Theatre, then he had to. The Fairy Godmother hugged him and as she did Jackson realised what he had done. And he felt sick to his stomach. But there was no going back now.

CHAPTER EIGHTEEN

Once the decision had been made that Jackson would narrate the play, he carried on with his explanation of the scenes from his scribbled script and everyone started to work out their positions on the stage. The Prince dramatically acted out how he would rail against being captured in the tower. Jackson watched him with amusement, thinking how theatrical the Prince was and how much more confident he was, even though he seemed to be about the same age. What Jackson didn't know was that someone else was watching just as closely. The Weasel lurked silent and sinister in the darkness of the foyer, peering with one sneaky eye through the crack between the doors to the auditorium. He held the front door key in the clenched fist of his right hand, having silently let himself in. In his other hand, he clutched a pile of bank notes that he had snatched from the till. Enough to keep the takings low but as always, not enough to be easily noticed. He had planned to go one step further tonight. He had planned to break into the Merry Theatre office and to empty the safe of everything. To cover his tracks carefully and to leave a few little bits of evidence. Just enough to point the finger of blame at Albert and Martha. But now, here he was and that pesky boy was on the stage with his friends. The Weasel had *assumed* that the theatre would be empty in the dead of night. He had *assumed* that his path would be clear and that he could be in and out of the Merry in minutes after completing his task. Why were all these children running around on the stage? What were they learning lines for? The more time stretched on as the Weasel stood watching, the more he seethed and the more he plotted his revenge for this inconvenient interruption to his plans.

The players had reached the final scene.

"And the gold confetti fluttered down over the trees, over the flowers, over the castle and over Puck. And as it did, she transformed before their eyes back into the beautiful, bright sprite she had always been," Jackson narrated as he imagined a narrator would. He grinned nervously at the Merry Players and realised with a flush of pride that in his role of narrator, he was now one of them. There was a pause, which made Jackson wonder what everyone was thinking. To his relief, they all started to applaud and whoop and cheer.

"It's brilliant!" Beauty enthused.

"Magical!" the Genie agreed.

"What shall we call it?" Jackson asked, looking down at his script that now had even more scribbles on it.

"Puck's Magical Mischief," Puck piped up.

"The King Saves The Day," the Prince suggested eagerly.

Beauty rolled her eyes, "How about The *Queen* Saves The Day?"

"The *Genie* Saves The Day!" the Genie chimed in cheekily.

Jackson could see a pattern emerging. The Fairy Godmother was looking up in to the rafters for inspiration.

"Fairy Godmother, what do you think?" Jackson prompted.

"The Cursed Castle?"

"I love it!" Beauty exclaimed.

"I think perhaps The King's Cursed Castle may sound better," the Prince announced unapologetically, determined to bring the focus back to himself.

Jackson was still thinking. "How about A Handful of Gold Confetti?" There were murmurings of approval. "Because in the end that's what it's all about really."

"A Handful of Gold Confetti, performed by The Merry Players!" the Genie looked out across the seats and swept his hand in front of his eyes as if he could see it up in lights. As Jackson followed his gaze, he noticed the foyer doors. Was one of them slightly open? He looked again. He must have been mistaken.

On the other side of the doors, the Weasel was as still as a statue. He continued to stare through the gap between them, unafraid. He would wait until this hideously happy troupe had gone and then set-about his dastardly deed. Jackson had left the stage to check the clock and came back in a fluster.

"It's already six o'clock! Quick! My parents will be up in a minute. I'll be in so much trouble if they know I've been in here again at night."

The friends gathered round him.

"Will we rehearse again tonight?" Beauty asked eagerly.

"We'll try. It's the last night of the show. But if I can't summon you after that, then I will get us together again as soon as I can. We need to plan when the show will be on and I need to make some posters to tell everyone and…"

"We can help you with all of that," the Fairy Godmother said sweetly. "And the show is fit for the stage already!"

The Weasel listened intently as their voices carried across

the auditorium. Summon them? What did the boy mean? Jackson delved into his pocket and pulled out the ring and the silk flower. He knelt down on the floor and opened the box gently.

"Puck. Beauty. You first, see you soon!" They said their goodbyes and as Jackson placed their props in the box, they disappeared instantly.

"Fairy Godmother and Prince, you're next," Jackson said as he picked up the wand and crown and added them to the pile.

They too vanished. The Weasel's mind was spinning at the sight. What *was* this? Magic? The children were there and then… Not there. He had never seen anything like it in all his dishonest days.

Lastly, Jackson looked down to pick up the lamp and only then did he realise that it wasn't where he had left it. His heart started drumming as he turned his head to see the Genie, several metres away, clutching the lamp to his chest.

"Just a little longer?" pleaded the Genie.

Jackson closed the box quickly and got to his feet, ready for a chase. The Weasel was transfixed.

"Genie, my Mum and Dad are going to be up any minute now! There's no time to mess around!" Jackson exclaimed marching across the stage.

"I won't get in the way. I just want to rehearse a bit more. I don't think I've quite got to grips with my lines yet. Could we go through the script again?" the Genie begged. "I want to make sure I get it right."

Jackson yawned, a big, exhausted yawn. "How am I going to explain you? Hey folks, this is my friend the Genie. Oh and by the way, Dad, he knows your grandparents and lives in this props box!"

By now Jackson was closer to his errant friend and was holding his hand out for the lamp. The Genie started walking slowly backwards, still refusing to give up the treasure.

"Magical props?" thought the Weasel. "That *live* in a box? And his parents don't know." His mind churned the new information over and over. He couldn't wait to tell his brother. The safe would have to wait. He wanted the box.

All of a sudden, the Genie bolted. Across the stage, down the stairs and into the seats. Jackson ran back to the box and scooped it up with both hands, in hot pursuit. The script! What about the script! He turned back to retrieve it. The Weasel, seeing the Genie racing towards him in a blur of bright blue and gold, scuttled across the foyer and crouched down behind the ticket desk. The Genie burst through the doors into the foyer, giggling cheekily with the lamp held tightly in his hand. He grappled with the front door lock and tumbled out into the street just as Jackson flung the foyer doors open and clutching the cumbersome box with his school bag swinging around him, followed the Genie outside, slamming the front door behind him. The Weasel stood up slowly and a sinister smirk spread across his face. He would wait until the coast was clear and then escape across the road to tell that bullish brother of his all about his delightful discoveries. By that night, not only would the box be theirs but Albert and Martha would be arrested. The Merry Theatre would be utterly destroyed.

Jackson found the Genie hiding around the corner. The morning sun slowly rose over the buildings.

"Ok, I've had a thought. As long as you promise to hide,

you can spend some time reading the script again but only if you give me a hand too." Jackson whispered as he ushered his gleeful friend into the courtyard.

"Of course, what do you need?"

"I need you to help me to get into the building across the road. I want to find out what's going on in there once and for all."

"Let's do it!" the Genie grinned as he whispered back.

Jackson smiled and urged his friend to keep quiet as they entered the house. They crept up the stairs. The Genie suppressed a giggle of excitement and Jackson threw him a warning look over his shoulder. In his room, he slid the treasure chest under the bed, once again pulling the covers down over the gap to hide it from view. Then they looked for the best place for the Genie to hide until his parents had gone across to the theatre. Jackson opened his wardrobe doors and moved a pile of clothes and some of his games to one side then signalled for the Genie to hurry inside. Seeing the look of reluctance on his face, Jackson stared at him sternly. The Genie rolled his eyes and stepped inside, his bright blue and gold outfit shining against Jackson's garments and the lamp still held tightly in his hand.

"And if you're going to be out of the box then you'll have to change into some of my clothes. If my Mum and Dad see you like that, they're going to wonder what on earth is going on. Please just be quiet until they've gone next door," Jackson whispered.

"Ok, I will act being the quietest boy in the world," the Genie grinned.

"And try to rub that moustache off!" Jackson exclaimed as he closed the door to, leaving the slightly offended Genie just enough light so he could sit quietly reading the script. Jackson sat down on the bed and suddenly felt overcome with such tiredness that he had to lie down and pull the covers over himself, falling asleep before his head had even hit the pillow.

CHAPTER NINETEEN

Jackson woke with a start. He sat up, realising that he was still fully dressed as he twisted towards his bedside table to check the time.

'Ten o'clock already,' he thought as the clock face came into focus and only then did he realise that someone was sitting cross-legged at the end of his bed. A boy dressed in one of his school shirts and a pair of his oldest trousers with his nose deep in the script, his hair flopping over his face and a smudge of face paint where his drawn-on moustache had been. The Genie. He looked so different out of his theatrical silks. Ordinary, just like one of Jackson's classmates.

"You're meant to be hiding!" Jackson stated, irritated that the Genie wasn't playing by the rules.

The Genie looked up from the pages, "Morning to you too," he said a little sarcastically and then, "Your Mum came in..."

"Did she see you?" Jackson interrupted, feeling panicky.

"No, no. Don't worry. She came in to check on you and then I heard her go downstairs and out of the front door. Your Dad too. Are these clothes alright? I feel a bit dowdy."

"You look just fine," Jackson reassured him. "If my parents ask, we'll say you're my school friend. They're too wrapped up in the theatre right now to know anyway."

He was keen to continue his investigations over the road and thought how nice it was to have a companion. He swung his legs over the side of the bed, realising he hadn't even taken his shoes off last night as he stood up to stretch. The Genie stood up too.

"Shall we run through the script together again?" he asked eagerly.

A glint of gold on the bedspread caught Jackson's eye. The lamp! He quickly grabbed it from the bed and held it behind his back. The Genie spun round realising that he was too late to grab it back. Before he could protest, Jackson spoke.

"I won't put it back in the box, I promise. Not yet. As I said, I want you to help me. But if I lose you or we get split up or get into any trouble, if I have the lamp, I can always help you to disappear."

The Genie thought for a moment, "What kind of trouble?"

"Let's go and find out." Jackson stuffed the lamp into his bag and slung it across him as he led the way out of the house.

As the two boys turned the corner and emerged out onto the street, Jackson couldn't believe what he saw. Workers in scruffy overalls were swarming around the front of the old town hall and the scaffolding was being taken down piece by piece. The top two thirds of the building were already revealed and the façade looked majestic in the morning sunlight. Passers-by stopped to watch as the impressive front doors were slowly revealed too. The doors had been painted the same black and gold as the ones inside that Jackson had seen through the window a couple of days ago. A sheet still covered the sign above them.

"Quickly," Jackson said, grabbing the Genie's arm and pulling him behind the postbox.

"What is it?" the Genie asked, watching as Jackson was transfixed by a couple who were walking towards the old town hall.

Mr Greengold in a smart suit and his trusty trilby hat clutched his briefcase as he approached the doors. His client walked alongside him wearing an expensive, long, red coat with a wide brimmed hat that certainly made her noticeable. Mr Greengold raised his hand to knock but the door swung open just as he did so and his hand fell down in front of him.

"Welcome!" Jackson heard the string-haired man bellow as he spat droplets of cold tea through his moustache and reached his hand towards his guests. "Ms Strudwick. I mean Lady Mayoress! Your reputation proceeds you, of course. How delightful to see you. And you must be Mr Greengold."

Mr Greengold shook the man's hand weakly. Jackson was curious to see that he simultaneously looked rather repulsed. "Good morning, Mr... Er...?"

"McCreedy! But just call me McCreedy, everyone does!" McCreedy roared. "And my brother, Walter."

The Weasel stepped out of the shadows and held a spindly, claw-like hand out by way of greeting.

"Lady Mayoress," McCreedy boomed, making everyone jump, "May I say, I have been so looking forward to meeting you and to showing you around your old stomping ground!"

Victoria Strudwick's eyes sparkled as she shook her new acquaintances' hands warmly. "Yes, likewise. I'm very intrigued to see what you've done with the old place."

"Come in, come in," McCreedy coaxed as he ushered them inside and the hefty doors closed heavily behind them.

Jackson watched, astonished. "They know each other!" he gasped, turning to the Genie. "That was Mr Greengold and the Weasel. They know each other!"

"Who was the lady in the hat?" the Genie asked.

"She's the Mayoress and the richest person in town. We have to get in there and hear what they're saying." Jackson started to walk quickly with the Genie in hot pursuit.

"How are we going to do that?"

Jackson stopped on the pavement and stared at the building. One of the workmen had just walked in and had left the door ajar. It was too good an opportunity to miss.

"Quick!" exclaimed Jackson and they walked hurriedly across the road, aiming straight for the door. Within moments they were inside, looking around nervously, as they realised the very workman who had just unwittingly let them in, now loomed over them.

"What are you boys up to?" he asked curiously.

The Genie thought more quickly than Jackson, "We're just waiting for my... er... Dad... He's just come in for a meeting. It's school holidays, see?"

The workman eyed him suspiciously but appeared to accept the explanation, striding back out the door and leaving them alone in the cavernous foyer. They stared at the sweeping staircase and plush décor.

"Where do you think they went?" the Genie whispered as Jackson tried to control his nerves.

"Maybe they're in the next room," he said, pointing to a set of doors and tiptoeing towards them, the immense portrait of the string-haired McCreedy looming over them. Jackson placed his hand on the door handle cautiously and pulled the door towards him, peering through the gap. His heart stopped at the sight. Rows and rows of uniform velvety chairs stretched out in front of his eyes. One glimpse was enough for him to know what this place was. It was a theatre. A brand new, spectacular theatre with no ripped carpet, no peeling paint, no dusty old chandelier and no money problems. His heart plummeted to the floor, his mouth was open. He was speechless. With no-one in sight on the other side, he opened the door a little further for his friend to see.

"Oh my goodness," the Genie whispered.

"It's a theatre," said Jackson feeling sick with the newness of everything. The carpet was even softer than it had looked. The shimmer of the immense chandelier practically blinded him when he looked up. The seats looked like you could curl up in them and sleep for a thousand years. The stage was vast and framed with luxurious, deep blue velvet curtains that were fringed with gold. Jackson stared in disbelief at the majestic grand circle that floated above the stalls. He thought of how devastated his parents were going to be when they found out the secret behind the scaffolding. How could the Merry Theatre ever compete?

"Come on, we have to find them and find out what on earth is going on!" Jackson whispered bravely as they darted inside to crouch behind the back row of chairs. They edged forwards, ducking in between rows and keeping their heads down below the backs of the seats.

Suddenly, McCreedy's fake laughter boomed out from the wings. Four figures stepped out into the limelight of the stage. Jackson and the Genie were only a few rows from the front and quickly threw themselves on the floor lying on their stomachs facing each other and holding their breath. The Genie stared at Jackson as if to say, "What now?"

"What now indeed," Jackson thought as he listened to the unfolding conversation.

"We have a full calendar of productions planned, starting with our gala opening night where the magnificent Serena Warblerina will be performing a one-off show to launch the theatre to a *distinguished* audience. And we will be introducing a new tenor to the stage, Harry Cuthbert. He is, without doubt, set to be the next big thing."

"Isn't he one of the Merry..." Mr Greengold started to say. McCreedy quickly talked over him, sweeping his hand across the view and turning the Mayoress' attention towards the stalls. "You will, *of course*, be our guest of honour."

The Mayoress nodded while Jackson fought back a gasp of horror. Harry? That was why he'd handed in his notice! That was why he had seen him on the street a couple of days ago. Harry was nothing but a wretched traitor!

Mr Greengold was scribbling notes furiously with an old-fashioned ink pen as the Weasel walked behind him in a blatant attempt to peer over his shoulder, sending a chill down his spine. Jackson carried on peering through the seats as the accountant tried to turn away from the spy. Victoria Strudwick was clearly impressed by the theatre but who wouldn't be? But Mr Greengold looked uneasy, as if he were doing a thousand calculations in his mind. The door from the foyer suddenly flew open and Jackson and the Genie heard the bustle of footsteps and the rustle of satin as someone rushed down the middle aisle.

"Oh goodness, I'm so sorry to interrupt!" said an anxious woman in a voice that was as familiar to Jackson as his own.

"I've brought Miss Warblerina's dress ready for her fitting this afternoon…" she trailed off as McCreedy glared at her.

"Well, put it in the dressing room, will you? Can't you see we are occupied with our guests?"

By now the voice had arrived at the front of the stalls and it's owner had stopped in her tracks. The loud rustling of material ceasing exactly in line with Jackson and his friend as they lay horrified and frozen to the spot staring up at her. The sight of them between the rows caught her eye and as she looked down her eyes met with Jackson's.

"Emma!" he mouthed in shock, only just managing to keep silent and then he shook his head, pleading with her not to react.

Emma frowned at him and then looked away quickly, stuttering, "Yes, yes, of course," to her boss and scuttling away as quickly as possible under the weight of Serena Warblerina's costume.

"Emma!" thought Jackson to himself. Another traitor! How could she? That's why she had been calling in sick. But there was no time to think. The group moved towards the front of the stage and footsteps thudded closer and closer towards their hiding place. Jackson shuffled backwards on his elbows and knees and the Genie, able to move more quickly going forwards looked at him desperately. The steps got closer. All the while McCreedy droning on about figures and finances and famous people, making Jackson want to jump up and scream at him to just SHUT UP.

"You see, investment in us is an investment in the future. Not like that pathetic little playhouse over the road. It's a money pit. A dead end. A Pointless. Waste. Of. Space," McCreedy leaned in towards the Mayoress' face as he walked alongside her, enunciating every word and breathing his putrid breath so that she had to lean back and walk with her back in an arch trying to avoid the spit that was flying from his mouth.

Jackson couldn't contain himself any more. The fury fizzed through him. Every thought in his head told him to stay down on the ground, to roll under the seats and hide but his heart was pounding so fiercely with anger that before he knew it he had scrambled to his feet.

"KINGBISCUITS!" he shouted at the top of his voice to summon his courage and the startled group turned to stare at him. Mr Greengold looked at him, bemused as he slowly realised who he was. Jackson thought he saw a flicker of pride on the man's face.

The Weasel recognised him straight away. "Well, if it isn't the Merry boy," he sneered under his breath. Victoria Strudwick stared at him baffled, trying to make sense of the interruption. The Weasel, thinking quickly, turned the confused Lady Mayoress and Mr Greengold away and led them back towards the stage and quickly into the wings.

"We'll leave them to their little chat," he said ominously as Mr Greengold looked back at Jackson with concern.

"Well, what the devil does the *Merry boy* think he is doing in MY THEATRE?" McCreedy hissed under his breath, lumbering towards him.

"You've got no right to talk about our theatre like that. We are not a waste of space. We are a... a wonderful... fantastic... brilliant, spectacular theatre and you can just... You can just... SHOVE OFF!" Jackson stammered, his whole body starting to freeze with fear.

"Shove off, you say? Like your father *shoved off* with MY

FORTUNE?" McCreedy spat.

"What? What... What do you mean?" Jackson stuttered edging backwards.

"That's right. Your pathetic little playhouse should have been MINE," McCreedy growled as Jackson started to back away. The man lurched towards him. "Interesting... Close up you really do look like your pathetic father. And you are obviously just as much of a WASTE. OF. SPACE."

The Genie was clambering to his feet, pulling himself up by grabbing onto the chair in front and stood between Jackson and McCreedy, bravely shielding his friend.

"I don't understand... I don't know what you're talking about..." Jackson's voice wobbled. The Genie stood firm as the man attempted to barge past him.

"Get out of my way, boy!" he shouted.

"No! Get out of my way! Or I will turn you into a mouse! I can do magic you know," the Genie replied confidently. "Alacadabrazam!" he said, waving an arm in McCreedy's face and watching curiously as he turned magenta with rage.

Jackson's mind was reeling. He watched his friend waving his arms throwing imaginary confetti over their adversary and just as he was about to speak McCreedy grabbed the Genie's arm. The Genie looked round at Jackson in alarm. "Run!" he shouted, "Use the lamp!"

Jackson knew exactly what his friend meant and span round, breaking into a run as he cleared the end of the row of seats. The Genie squirmed in McCreedy's tightening grip.

"LET ME GO!" he protested.

"Not until you tell me EXACTLY what you are doing in MY theatre," McCreedy leant menacingly close to the Genie and then glanced over his shoulder as Jackson clattered through the doors into the foyer.

"STOP THAT BOY!" he shouted at no one in particular, knowing that he was already gone. He turned back to his captive, twisting his arm as he hissed, "So, boy. Tell me."

"Well... Um... It's nothing really. We just... Well..."

"Spit. It. Out."

"Just, you know, curiosity. You know what kids are like?" the Genie said with a nervous smile, wondering if he could charm his way out of this after all.

"Curiosity? Do I come into your house because I am *curious*?" There was a pause. "Well, *do I*?"

"I am guessing... No?" the Genie said cheekily, feeling braver and braver as he knew that Jackson would be getting closer and closer to the props box with the lamp. He was right. Jackson had burst out of the front doors of the shiny, new theatre, running straight into one of the workmen as he did.

"Sorry, sorry!" he wheezed as he carried on running, tripping over his own feet. He ran on, his legs falling from under him, into the courtyard, into the house, up the stairs, bursting into his bedroom and throwing himself onto the floor, scrabbling around for the box, relieved to find it where he had left it. He tore at his bag, delving into it for the lamp and threw it into the open box with a clatter. Only then did he stop to catch his breath and just as he was about to take the lamp back out to check the Genie was ok, he realised his Mum and Dad were standing at the door looking at him.

"Are you alright Jackson?" his Mum asked.

Over the road McCreedy stood in shock looking at his empty hands, wondering what on earth had just happened. Wondering how the boy, who was cowering before him just moments ago, had vanished into thin air.

"You've got to come with me, quickly," Jackson said as he closed the box without explanation. He got to his feet and grabbed his Dad by his shirtsleeve, tugging at his arm as he left the room. "Come on, you've got to see this."

Albert and Martha followed their son down the stairs, taking them two at a time and practically running down the alleyway until they were looking at the old town hall.

"What is it Jackson? What's so desperate?" his Dad asked and as he did so, he looked up to see the workmen removing the covering from the sign over the entrance. The gold swirling letters revealed to the world. 'GRAND THEATRE' it read.

"Theatre," Jackson's parents read out loud in unison. Theatre. Albert looked down at his son, crushed. Another two workmen were positioning gold-framed posters on either side of the doors. A picture of a glamorous woman with piercing blue eyes and a head full of cascading brown curls wearing a magnificent, midnight blue dress stared back at them. 'Opening Night. An Exclusive Evening with Serena Warblerina,' the text read with the date emblazoned across the bottom of each one. The date was tomorrow. Albert strained his eyes to read the smaller text underneath the soprano's name, 'Accompanied by Harry Cuthbert.'

Jackson looked as his Dad swayed in the street, looking light-headed and sick. His Mum was as white as a sheet. "Oh Harry," she said.

"It's a theatre," his Dad whispered.

Finally, Albert found his voice. He looked at Martha. "So, it looks like tonight really might be our last night."

He turned to Jackson. "I had hoped you would run the theatre one day, son." Jackson saw there were tears in his Dad's eyes as he stared back across the road.

"You can't just give up Dad! We've got to put on a good show haven't we?"

"But... Harry. I can't believe it... Harry."

Jackson thought for a moment. He thought about how his friends had encouraged him. "Now, more than ever, you have to play his role!"

His Dad looked him in the eye. "I haven't been on the stage for years, Jackson, you know that."

"But you know every line. You know every bit of that role. You can easily step into Harry's shoes!"

"He's right, Albert," his Mum said knowingly. "Jackson can look after the lights, can't you Jackson?"

"I can. I won't get it wrong, Dad. I promise. I won't get distracted."

"I know Jackson, I'm sorry I was so hard on you. I suppose it's about time I acted on my own stage again. And I suppose you'll find out sooner or later. Mr Greengold, the man your Mum and I have been having meetings with, well, he was trying to find us an investor, so there is still a bit of hope."

Jackson was amazed, was his Dad finally trusting him with the truth?

"He knows the Lady Mayoress, Victoria Strudwick and apparently she is looking to buy a new business. She's coming to see the show tonight so I'll make sure I act my socks off!"

Jackson really wanted to be enthusiastic for his parents' sake but couldn't hide the truth from them.

"I saw Victoria Strudwick. And Mr Greengold. They were going into the Grand with the owners and talking about her investing there."

Albert took in his son's words, "Oh." He said in a small voice.

He knew exactly what this meant. If Victoria was going to put her money into the Grand, why would she want to buy another theatre? "Well, it looks like this *will* be our last show after all."

"And the owners, they seem to know you." Jackson watched his Dad's expression change.

"What do you mean?"

Jackson knew he had to confess. "I went inside... And they saw me..."

Martha looked exasperated. "Jackson! What has got into you lately? You're sneaking into our theatre in the middle of the night, almost getting caught up in a break-in and now you're sneaking into other people's property!"

"It doesn't matter!" Jackson blurted out. "They know you! They said that our theatre, the Merry, should have been..."

"Jackson, it *does* matter. You really need to start being more responsible. Can't you see how much we've got to deal with here? This isn't time for childish games." His Dad turned to walk away and his Mum followed, "Come on Jackson, don't just stand there."

"He said the Merry should have been theirs..." Jackson called after them but they weren't listening.

CHAPTER TWENTY

Jackson bounded up the stairs. He needed to talk to his friends. Now. And he needed to check that the Genie had survived his encounter with the string-haired bully McCreedy. He had left the box by his bed when his parents had surprised him earlier and his stomach turned at the thought of how he hadn't hidden it. What was he thinking? What with the break-in and knowing about the villains across the road, he resolved to keep the box with him at all times from now on as he threw the lid open and grabbed at the props. The Genie appeared first, looking rather stunned. He looked around and quickly realised he was back in the safety of Jackson's bedroom.

"Jackson!" he said, throwing his arms around him with relief. The others appeared one by one. Ting, ting, ting, ting!

"Is it show time?" Puck asked, striking a pose, her tufty hair looking… well, tufty. Jackson gulped as Beauty looked at him apprehensively.

"What's the matter?" the Fairy Godmother asked as she sat down on the floor beside him.

"There isn't going to be a show," Jackson said heavily, setting off a series of gasps and exclamations around the room.

"Why not?" Puck asked, pouting and dropping down with a thump to sit crosslegged on the floor.

"My parents are closing the Merry. They don't have a choice." And Jackson told them all about the flashy new theatre across the road and how they didn't stand a chance of surviving against such competition. When he had finished talking, he saw his friends all staring back at him in disbelief.

"But what about our show? We can help your Mum and Dad," Beauty said hopefully.

"It won't be enough. We're in masses of debt. More than you can imagine. And our last hope of investment is lost. It's over."

No one spoke. Even the usually energetic Genie wasn't sure what to do. The Prince, who had been surprisingly quiet, now stepped forwards.

"So you're just going to roll over and surrender?" he snapped.

Jackson looked at him, a little taken aback. "I'm not just rolling over. We've tried!"

"What have we *tried*? We haven't even put our show on yet!"

Jackson, starting to feel rather ruffled, stood up and looked the Prince straight in the eyes. "You don't know anything about it! My Mum and Dad have been trying for years. They've really worked at this place. You haven't even *seen* the theatre across the road. It's MASSIVE! It's literally called the GRAND. They've got a MASSIVE world-class star headlining their MASSIVE opening night tomorrow. We're just the Merry Players. There's no way we can compete."

"*Just* the Merry Players?" the Genie sounded hurt.

"You know what I mean!" Jackson said exasperated. "You saw the place!"

"We're not *JUST* the Merry Players," the Prince seethed. "You just summon us up on a whim and now you're *giving up*? I can't believe you're being so... so... cowardly."

Jackson could feel his anger bubbling up through his body.

All the anger he felt towards the Weasel and McCreedy for wanting to destroy their home. Towards Mr Greengold for introducing the Mayoress to their competition. Towards Emma and Harry for being such traitors and towards his Mum and Dad for never listening to a word he said. It all swirled around inside him like a potion in a bubbling cauldron.

"Are you calling me a coward?" he challenged.

By now the others were all on their feet too.

"Calm down, both of you," said the Genie.

This annoyed Jackson even more, he didn't want to calm down. He glared at the Prince. "Are you?"

The Prince hesitated for a moment, then said, "Yes, I am. You coward!" With that he drew his sword from his belt and Puck gasped.

"GLASSAPPLE!" Jackson roared and ran at the Prince, knocking the sword out of his hand and pushing him back against the wall. The Prince let out a growl and grabbed at Jackson's leg, trying to lift it from the floor to make him lose his footing. The boys spun around and the others scattered, making room for their fight, not knowing how to intervene.

"Come on Jackson!" shouted Beauty as the Genie looked at her with surprise and Puck jumped on to the bed to get a better view.

Jackson hopped backwards and seized the Prince's arm, spinning around and somehow twisting it behind his back.

"Say SORRY!" he shouted, knowing his parents were out of earshot but not caring at all if they heard him.

"No! You coward!" The Prince kicked at Jackson's shins like a mule and tipped forwards trying to unbalance him.

"Take that back!" Just as Jackson thought he was winning the fight, he toppled and the Prince threw a punch at his arm shouting, "Argh!"

Jackson took the hit and aimed straight back at the Prince's side, closing his eyes and waiting to feel the impact on his fist. Which is why he was amazed when he felt nothing but thin air.

There was a clattering noise. As Jackson opened his eyes he saw that only the Fairy Godmother remained in the room, looking rather pleased with herself as she dropped the ring and therefore, Beauty, back into the box.

"I thought you needed a break," she smiled.

Jackson stood with his hands on his knees getting his breath back. He looked up at his friend, "I'm not a coward."

"I know," the Fairy Godmother said kindly.

Jackson continued, sounding more like he was trying to convince himself more than her. "I haven't got a choice. What can a bunch of little kids like us do?"

"We're not so little. The first Merry Players show I was in had a full house. Your great-grandma was so proud of us, I remember her standing at the side of the stage clapping louder than anyone." The Fairy Godmother looked wistful for a moment and seemed older than her years.

"What's she like?" Jackson asked.

"So enthusiastic, a bit like your Dad I imagine. She's always so proud of your great-grandad. They're always there for each other."

"Like my Mum is always there for my Dad." Jackson felt tears welling up in his eyes and quickly shooed them away with the back of his hand.

The Fairy Godmother stood up and put her arms around Jackson, in a way that reminded him of his Mum's hugs.

When they let go of each other, the Fairy Godmother's eyes

were sparkling, "We could put our show on anyway?"

"When?"

"I don't know… Tomorrow! While the Grand is having its opening night," she smiled at the thought.

Jackson stood up straight and felt a smile appear on his face. "A final act of defiance!" he said sounding like he was quoting from one of his books.

The Fairy Godmother was thinking. "The press will be there for the opening won't they? Taking pictures and making sure the story is in the papers?"

"Yes, they're bound to be," Jackson replied, slowly catching up with her thoughts as she grinned at him. "We've got a good story for them. They've stolen our actors. And taken our investor!"

"Exactly! And putting on our show will let them know we aren't just giving in."

"That's brilliant!" Jackson was excited. If the Merry was going down, they weren't going down without a fight! He just had to convince his Mum and Dad to let him put on their play before the theatre closed. "I'd better go and talk to my parents," Jackson announced and the Fairy Godmother picked up the wand, knowing what she had to do next.

She gave Jackson one more hug, "I'll see you later!" And with that she placed the wand in the box herself and immediately vanished.

Across the courtyard and inside the Merry Theatre, Jackson crept into the wings and watched as Albert and Seamus paced around the stage. Having resolved to keep the treasure chest with him at all times, the box was now at his feet, its secrets hidden within. His Dad clutched the script in his hand and looked proudly out into the theatre as he delivered his lines. He seemed almost giddy, as if he had completely forgotten the reason he had to play Harry's part. Jackson thought about how he would have to perform the next day. He knew it would be easy to persuade his Mum and Dad to let him do it, they would be thrilled to see their son on the stage but butterflies came to life in Jackson's stomach when he thought about himself standing in his Dad's shoes. And as the butterflies fluttered and flapped more and more wildly he felt more and more dizzy, until he had to crouch on the floor, leaning on the wooden box for support and wondering how on earth he was going to do it.

CHAPTER TWENTY-ONE

The night arrived too quickly and the atmosphere was sombre backstage. Albert had gathered the actors and ushers together as soon as they had arrived and Jackson watched as he addressed them with a trembling voice and tears in his eyes. There were gasps and sighs as they all took in the news. Across the road, the Grand was in darkness, its garish entrance waiting in anticipation for the opening the following night. The Merry staff had seen it for the first time as they arrived for work. The shockwaves were still ricocheting around the dressing rooms as they prepared themselves for their last show. Louisa once again stepped into Emma's shoes and over-sized dress as Emma had called in sick once again, not having the courage to admit that she had already jumped ship.

Ironically, that evening's show had sold out and the seats would be full even if the Merry's pockets were still empty. The audience were gathering, gossiping about the shiny new theatre across the road. If Jackson had been listening he would have heard some of the finer gentlemen and their elegant wives boasting about how they had been invited to the press opening the very next night. Even the invitation hadn't mentioned that it was a theatre, simply referring to the launch as a spectacular surprise. But Jackson was sitting backstage, with the props box on his lap, listening as his Dad rehearsed his lines over and over again. He had decided to wait until after the show to ask about his plan. He saw for the first time evidence of butterflies fluttering around inside his Dad and it occurred to him that even his Dad had his own fears to face when it came to being on stage.

The bell rang to signal to the audience that it was time to take their seats. Chivalrous men invited their wives to take their places first and the ladies sidled along the rows in their dresses, flipping down their seats and settling in, chocolates on their laps and anticipation on their faces. The actors made final preparations and hustled and bustled their way to the side of the stage.

"There you are!" Martha exclaimed, appearing by her nervous husband's side. "Have you forgotten? Mr Greengold is waiting."

It was obvious to Jackson that his Dad had completely forgotten that he had made arrangements to meet with Mr Greengold and Victoria Strudwick before the show. Jackson saw little point now that it was clear that the Mayoress was interested in the Grand but his parents were far too well-mannered to ignore the lady. And so, with his mind full of his lines and his heart full of sorrow, Albert followed his wife to go and meet his guests. Jackson followed quietly behind them and hid behind the door listening as his parents greeted Victoria Strudwick warmly. The Mayoress' teeth sparkled like diamonds as she beamed back at Albert and Martha. Mr Greengold faded into the background in the presence of three such charismatic people.

"You have the best seats in the house!" Jackson heard his Mum exclaim.

"Marvellous! It's a wonderful place you have here, I'll be watching the performance with interest," Victoria enthused.

"It's very kind of you to come, Ms Strudwick. Especially as I understand your interests now lie… Elsewhere…" his Dad added.

There was a pause as Victoria slowly understood what Albert meant. Mr Greengold was about to interrupt but the Mayoress spoke, gently placing her arm on Mr Greengold's arm to hush him.

"One must never express one's interests until one understands exactly what one is interested in, as they say."

Albert remained silent, unsure how to respond.

"What on earth was she talking about?" thought Jackson. It was obvious her interests were across the road.

"Well, we'd best get backstage, Albert's standing in tonight," Martha said, suddenly realising the audience were nearly all settled and they left their guests to take their seats in the low, magical light.

Jackson rushed away from the door and headed to the lighting panel. He looked across at the wing, thinking of all the times Harry had swept past him in and out of scenes, ruffling his hair. A silence fell as Albert stepped out into the spotlight. A couple in the front row who had been coming to the Merry for years recognised him and started applauding. The audience around them followed suit and the applause rippled through the theatre getting louder and louder until Albert found himself simply smiling and soaking up the moment. As the claps died down, Jackson watched his Dad with a mixture of sadness and pride as he began to speak.

"Before our performance begins tonight, I need to make an announcement." He paused and took a deep breath. "It is with great sorrow and regret that I must announce that this will be our last ever show. We have had many happy years here and my grandparents had many happy years before us but, unfortunately, we must accept the upkeep of such a wonderful theatre is beyond us and we must sadly close our doors for the final time tonight."

Albert looked out to the sad and shocked faces that now looked back at him. His eyes settled on Mr Greengold who looked at him, puzzled. He had not been expecting such an announcement at all and glanced at Victoria Strudwick to see what she was making of it. The Mayoress looked deep in thought.

"Thank you for being such magnificent supporters of our little theatre all these years," Albert continued, his voice cracking with emotion. "Oh and tonight, I'll be doing my best to play Harry Cuthbert's role. Enjoy the show!" he managed to add.

With that he left the stage to another round of applause led by his own actors, barely managing to stop himself from crying as they crowded around and hugged him. If Jackson or any one of them had turned their head at that moment, they would have seen the figure of a weaselly-looking handyman in overalls with a spindly stuck-on moustache, standing there, listening to every word before sneaking by in the darkness and disappearing up the stairs into the Merry Theatre office. The creak of the floorboards drowned out by the sound of the applause.

CHAPTER TWENTY-TWO

The Weasel sniffed around the office. A heavy, mahogany desk stood in the middle of the room, scattered with papers, pens and scripts, in contrast to the ordered wooden shelves that decorated the wall behind. The shelves were full of programmes from previous shows, all filed neatly in date order, a clear illustration of just how long the Merry had been running. And then on the bottom shelf, files full of paperwork, records of income and outgoings. The Weasel rifled through them hungrily, taking in the minus figures and question marks scribbled in Albert's own writing. He started to smirk. His miserable plan had been working. Snatching those bank notes from the cash drawer night after night had left Albert utterly confused. The Weasel couldn't believe his luck. Had he really just heard Albert announce that the theatre would be closing after tonight? This was more than he could ever have hoped for. But there was more. Curled up in the corner, there it was, forgotten and frayed, the rope from the fallen set. The rope that the Weasel had cut. His intention had been simply to hide a bag of notes in the office and then call the police to tip them off, framing Albert and Martha for hiding their takings and being dishonest with their accounts. But now he had the chance to pull off something much bigger. Albert had planted the evidence himself. The fool! The rope guiltily hidden, after being tampered with. And the Weasel had everything he needed to bring Albert and Martha down in front of their audience, to ruin their reputation and to shame them in plain view of the entire town. And all on the very last night of the Merry Theatre. He could make it a night that nobody would ever forget. A grand finale that even his brother would have to commend him for.

Running his weaselly paws along the shelf, he searched for the right spot to put the money. And then he knew. The programmes. He opened his bag, which was bursting with notes that he had systematically stolen from the cash drawer in the Merry foyer. And then stuffed them, a large handful in each, inside the pages of programme after programme on the shelf. He moved quickly with the muffled sounds of laughter and applause from the audience in the background. And then the task was complete, the programmes back on the shelf, concealing their evidence. He knew he should leave and make the phone call from across the road but how could he miss such a glorious moment? So he sat in Albert's own chair at Albert's own desk and picked up the receiver of Albert's own telephone and dialled the number slowly with a satisfied smile.

"Sergeant Goodman?" he croaked, disguising his voice.

"Speaking," the Sergeant confirmed.

"I have reason to believe that Albert and Martha Merry have been dishonest about their takings and have committed fraud. The money..."

Sergeant Goodman couldn't believe what he was hearing, "Sir, that is a rather serious accusation," he interrupted. "Can I please take your name..."

The Weasel paid no attention to the policeman, "The missing money is hidden in the programmes in their office. And furthermore, I would encourage you to ask Albert Merry about the rope that he has hidden by his desk. Mark my words, the set falling was no accident. I would suggest that it was a deliberate act of sabotage so that they can make a false insurance claim. I have it on good authority that the Merrys are planning to disappear after their final show this evening. You should arrest them before they have the chance to escape."

And with that, the Weasel replaced the receiver with a deliberate click, leaving Sergeant Goodman lost for words but with no choice but to reach for his search warrant and to rush to the Merry Theatre to investigate. Meanwhile, the temptation to see the resulting fall out was too much for the Weasel. Even if he was in disguise as Wilf, he knew it was too risky to loiter in the corridor and impossible to hide in the office. He waited for another roar from the audience to cover up the creaks as he crept down the stairs and then turned right into the props room. Amongst the dust sheets and boxes, this was the perfect spot to hide.

He didn't have to wait long. The sound of the siren in the street made the back few rows of the audience shuffle uncomfortably, some of them turning to look, as if they were able to see through the walls out onto the street. Jackson, who had been intensely focused on the lighting cues, heard the crash as Sergeant Goodman burst through the doors of the theatre. Jackson's Mum dashed out of the wardrobe room and appeared in the wing, flustered and together they peered out onto the stage.

"What on earth is going on?" she asked.

"Official police business, please stop the show immediately!" Sergeant Goodman announced as he charged down the aisle. Albert and Seamus, who were in the middle of an amusing exchange on stage, stopped mid-line to turn and stare out into the darkness. The faces of the crowd turned one by one, jaws falling like dominos as Sergeant Goodman passed them. Albert tried to shade his eyes from the lights, disorientated as he peered out to locate the policeman.

"Sergeant Goodman?" he queried, as Seamus stood next to him with his hands on his hips, confused and indignant.

"Could we talk in private please, Albert?" the Sergeant said in low tones as he approached the stage.

"Sergeant, I don't know if you've noticed but we're rather in the middle of something."

The policeman removed his hat and mopped his brow with a handkerchief, hot in the stage lights and aware of the hundreds of eyes staring at the back of his head and ears all craning to hear their conversation.

"That's quite apparent, Albert. But you have been accused of fraudulent behaviour and a deliberate act of sabotage and I must insist that you allow me to search your office immediately."

The Sergeant held his search warrant out and Albert edged towards the front of the stage to peer at it. He looked up at the audience apologetically, mortified that this was happening in front of them. His eyes settled on the Mayoress. Their chances really were blown now, he thought as the reality of the situation dawned on him once again and his heart fell into his shoes.

"I've got to tell you Sergeant, this is rather unorthodox," he mumbled under his breath and then straightened himself up to address the audience. "I can only apologise. Please bear with us, while we have a five minute interval. Ice creams are available in the foyer."

Whispers turned to frantic chatter and Seamus stared at Albert in astonishment as Sergeant Goodman made his way onto the stage and led him away to the office. As Martha turned and disappeared into the corridor, Jackson instinctively started to follow his Dad and before he realised it, he was standing on the side of the stage, forgetting himself for a moment and only realising when he felt the eyes of the audience all turn to him at once. The sight made him scuttle back into the wing and he felt a familiar feeling of nausea and fear.

As the actors gathered in the wing, waiting, Jackson *had* to know what was going on. He scooped the box up in his arms and ran down the corridor, pushing past anyone in his way. The door of the office was closed but that didn't stop him bursting in.

"What's going on?" Jackson demanded as he fell through the door. In front of him, the Sergeant was looking sorrowfully at a pile of theatre programmes spread out on the desk, each with money spilling from their pages. Martha was aghast, pulling programmes from the shelf, one after another, opening them and watching notes fall to the floor. Albert stood watching, frozen to the spot.

"I just don't… I didn't… I…" he muttered to himself, panicked, his face reddening. He looked up at Jackson, "Not now, Jackson!"

Jackson stepped back in shock at the fury in his Dad's eyes. "But I…" he stumbled.

"Close. The. Door!" his Dad demanded.

He did as commanded, tears in his eyes. He knew exactly what to do and ran down the steps, turning a sharp right into the props room. He would hear every word from in there. He placed the props box carefully at his feet and crouched next to it, listening intently to every word between his parents and Sergeant Goodman. If he had only listened a little more closely to his surroundings, he would have realised that only a few feet away was the sound of laboured breath as the Weasel hid under a dust sheet, waiting.

The voices drifted through the grate as they had done when Jackson first discovered the box.

"That's pure insanity, Sergeant. Of course I didn't tamper with the rope!" Albert stated, sounding increasingly agitated.

"Well, somebody has, Albert. The evidence is here. Look, you know I consider you to be friends. I don't want to but I'm going to have to do this officially. These accusations are very serious," the Sergeant said with a sombre tone. There was the sound of metal clinking. The sound of two pairs of handcuffs clicking shut. "Albert Jack Merry and Martha Frances Merry, I arrest you on suspicion of fraudulent behaviour. You do not have to say anything but whatever you do say may be written down and used in evidence against you."

"I will say something. We haven't done anything!" Martha exclaimed. "We've done nothing but love this theatre for years."

"Why would we hide money from our own business? Why would we deliberately harm our own staff? It doesn't make any sense!" Albert's anger burst through the grate and Jackson heard footsteps as the group made their way towards the door and out into the corridor.

Martha protested, "This is ridiculous! We're in the middle

of a show! You know us, Sergeant. Of course, we haven't done this. What happened to innocent until proven guilty?"

Jackson jumped up. He couldn't just let his parents be arrested. He burst into the corridor, which was full of people. Seamus, Louisa, even Stanley the head usher, all of the actors, all confused, all asking questions. Sergeant Goodman had his hand firmly on Albert's shoulder and was silently guiding him through the crowd while Albert railed and shouted, his hands cuffed firmly behind his back. "We're not thieves! This is absolute madness!"

Jackson followed the group. "Mum! Dad!" He felt panicked. Everything was out of control. Outside, the Sergeant led Albert and Martha to the front of the building. Jackson was hurrying alongside them, "Where is he taking you, Mum?"

A large number of the audience had made their way outside, curious as to what they could see and the noise of the whispers increased as the Merrys appeared in the light of the front of the building. Mr Greengold looked on with confusion while the Mayoress remained tight-lipped, taking in the scene with her usual composure.

"Where is he taking you?" Jackson repeated.

"To the police station. For questioning," Sergeant Goodman said flatly. "It would really be best if you stay here, Jackson. Who can look after your boy, Albert? Martha?"

Martha looked around, clearly overwhelmed. "Seamus? Louisa? Can Jackson come home with you?"

"Yes, yes, of course," Seamus answered.

"It will all be ok, Jackson, I promise. Stay with Seamus!" his Mum called.

Jackson stood for a moment. Just until there was no one looking at him and then he didn't stay to hear any more. He needed to speak to his friends and he had gone cold all over when he realised that he had left the box in the props room unguarded. His heart racing he ducked and dived through the crowd, away from Seamus, away from Louisa, running the length of the building back to the side door. If he had looked to his right as he burst in, he would have been just in time to see a weaselly figure scampering out into the auditorium clutching a wooden box. A magical wooden box that he couldn't believe had just been sitting on the floor unguarded when he had removed the sheet that had been covering him.

Jackson practically fell into the props room and threw himself on the floor where the box had been.

"No, no, no," he repeated over and over, tears spilling from his eyes, "No, no, no!"

CHAPTER TWENTY-THREE

Having hidden the box in the Grand Theatre office, the Weasel joined his brother on the pavement. The crowd had subsided a little and he noticed that Stanley, the ancient usher was standing guard at the front doors like an ill-equipped watchman.

"You seem to have caused quite a stir, Walter," McCreedy said under this breath, refusing to congratulate his brother.

"And you thought I wouldn't do it," the Weasel snarled back.

"Keep your voice down," McCreedy hissed through his teeth.

Directly in front of them, Micky Taleteller was busy questioning some of the stunned audience members who had had their evening of theatre transformed into a drama of epic proportions. The Weasel recognised him having seen his photograph against articles in the local paper. He knew that Micky made it his business to know everything about everyone even before they knew it about themselves. He watched as Micky scurried about talking to anyone who was willing to be interviewed. The Weasel nudged his brother and nodded in the journalist's direction. Micky suddenly became aware of a rather imposing figure standing on the edge of the kerb, calmly smoking a cigar, rocking on his heels as if he was about to topple over. It struck Micky that his hair looked a lot like wet string. And next to him a sliver of a man, with a long body, short legs and sharp pointy features, who looked like he might blow over in the breeze.

As Micky approached, McCreedy tried to hide his smug smile and rearranged his expression into one of concern, only managing to look like he had just eaten a bad prawn. Micky stretched his hand out and introduced himself, wincing as the man blew a cloud of cigar smoke in his face as he said his name.

"Greedy?" Micky enquired as he scribbled on his notepad. He knew how important detail was.

"MCCREEDY!" the man spat. "And this is my brother Walter." The Weasel nodded but didn't offer his hand. "Terrible business."

Micky looked up to see his interviewee nodding towards the Merry Theatre and realised what he meant.

"Oh yes, terrible. The place is an institution. Been there for years. What's your connection with the theatre?" he asked, suddenly quite intrigued.

McCreedy rocked forwards on the kerb. "No connection, just a..." he paused for a moment, "... concerned neighbour." He curled his lip around the word 'concerned', not sounding concerned at all.

Micky replied with another question, "Do you live locally?"

McCreedy plunged his hand into his inside pocket and rummaged around for a moment before pulling out a business card with ostentatious gold lettering. He handed it over and Micky realised how grubby his fingernails were, like a year's worth of grime was compressed underneath them. 'MR AUGUSTUS MCCREEDY, DIRECTOR,' the card read.

"Right. Director of...?" Micky asked politely, wondering if

there was more information written in invisible ink.

"This rather impressive establishment behind me." With that McCreedy stepped down from the kerb and yanked Micky's arm to turn him towards the Grand.

The Weasel watched in silence as the reporter was forced to look at the magnificent building. Micky had noticed it when he had arrived at the Merry but hadn't really taken it in in all its grandiosity. He tipped his head so far back that his trilby hat nearly fell off of his head, managing to grab it with his free hand just in time.

"Impressive," Micky admitted. "You must be very upset for your fellow theatre owner then, Sir?"

"Upset? Oh, of course. Terrible business," he said again. Micky realised that he was now being walked, or rather pushed, towards the Grand by McCreedy with the Weasel creeping silently along beside them with more than a hint of menace. Micky felt like digging his heels into the ground. The smell of stale cigar smoke and day-old coffee enveloped him as the man continued to speak.

"You're obviously a man who has a nose for a good story. You'll be at our opening night tomorrow of course. Our star, Miss Serena Warblerina will be taking interviews on the red carpet before the show. I can guarantee you a prime position for an exclusive."

Micky stared at the poster in front of him, a glamorous woman with steely eyes and a head full of cascading curls stared back at him. He recognised her from theatre reviews in London. An exclusive like this would guarantee him a front page.

"Fantastic," he replied enthusiastically, knowing he had no choice but to accept the offer.

McCreedy released his grip and slapped him on the back with a thud, "Good man!" he boomed, tapping the ash from his cigar.

The Weasel had heard enough and marched towards the Grand's ornate doors with his brother in tow. Micky was left staring at the cigar ash that had floated down on to his shoe.

Inside the Merry Theatre, Jackson was amid dust sheets and boxes waiting. He wiped the back of his hand across his hot forehead, tears still on his cheeks. He felt dizzy. The background noise of the last people leaving the auditorium sounded muffled. He could hear Seamus shouting his name and pacing up and down the corridor. A mix of other voices chattered, some calling his name, others discussing the events of the night.

"What are they supposed to have done?"

"Taken money."

"Maybe that's why Harry and Emma left, maybe they knew?"

"Don't be ridiculous, Albert and Martha would never do something like that."

"Albert has been acting strangely though. Martha hasn't been herself lately. And the decision to close the theatre seems so sudden. Maybe it's all a scam and they've got plans to run off with all the cash."

Jackson wanted to burst out into the corridor to stop the gossip but knew he couldn't risk being discovered. He needed to wait for the theatre to be empty so that he could search for the box. He needed his friends around him. How could the box just go missing? He knew exactly where he'd left it. Who would have even been in the room? As his panic spiralled, he lifted sheets, moved props and found himself checking his

159

pockets. As if the box could have shrunk and fallen into one of them. Suddenly, he became aware of Seamus' voice again. "I'll check the props room!"

Jackson scrambled to the back of the room and quickly dived on to the floor, pulling sheets and boxes on top of him. The door smashed against the wall as Seamus burst in.

"Jackson!" he shouted. "Where are you?"

Jackson screwed his eyes up tightly and stayed completely still, not daring to breathe. Seamus looked around, moving a few of the closest props but quickly gave up, deciding that there was nowhere in here for his friends' son to hide. As soon as the door closed, Jackson threw the sheets back and gulped in some air. He could hear Seamus agreeing with Louisa that they should check the house, followed by the sound of hurried footsteps then the slam of a door. Jackson listened for a moment to be certain that he was alone. Nothing. He waited. Suddenly his knees buckled and he fell heavily to the floor. His breath stopped for the briefest moment and then settled into a steady rhythm as exhaustion took over and he fell into a deep sleep.

CHAPTER TWENTY-FOUR

Jackson's eyes pinged open like a doll being tipped backwards. His body felt heavy and rested. Sun was streaming in to the room so he must have been asleep for hours. He knelt up and looked around him and then he remembered. Sergeant Goodman. The final show. His parents being arrested. The box. His friends. Everything from the night before tumbled back into his mind. Maybe the box was somewhere else in the theatre? Maybe someone had just put it somewhere safe? It just didn't make sense. He had left the box on the floor. There was no reason that anyone would have been in the props room with all the action that had been going on front of house and backstage. Or maybe someone *had* been in there?

Jackson stepped cautiously in to the corridor. It was completely silent. He was still feeling a bit dizzy and realised he hadn't eaten anything since yesterday afternoon. His Mum had promised him an ice cream in the interval but... He pictured his parents now, sitting on iron bunk beds, in striped outfits, eating crusts of bread. But there was no time for tears. Surely Seamus and Louisa were still looking for him and surely they would come back to the theatre to search. He had to have a look around the office, for the props box and to find something that would prove his Mum and Dad's innocence. The stairs creaked loudly and for once Jackson didn't care. He bounded up them two at a time, thudding on the wooden floorboards and burst into the room. The theatre programmes were strewn across the desk with money spilling from their pages. Jackson pulled books from the shelves and opened every drawer. He crawled on the floor to look under the cupboards and stood on the desk chair to look on top of them. There was no sign of the box anywhere.

Jackson slumped down in his Dad's chair, his chin on his chest, his legs dangling. He'd looked everywhere. Suddenly, he sat bolt up right on the edge of the chair. The slim drawer under the desktop! He tried the handle. The drawer was locked. The box would never fit in there of course but Jackson was curious. What did his parents have locked away? Jackson had no idea where to find the key. It was probably on his Dad's key ring. What could he use to break it open? A bronze letter opener caught his eye, just the thing! Jackson slid the end of the letter opener into the crack at the top of the drawer and pushed up against the underside of the desktop. Ping! It slipped and he was thrown forwards on to the desk. But he wasn't in the mood to be defeated and immediately made another attempt. He could feel the lock being pushed down. The wood was old and weak. CRACK! The wood split as the lock released and the drawer was open. It was full of old, faded paperwork in a bulging, dusty, beige folder and a selection of newspaper cuttings that he had never laid eyes on before. He grabbed at the folder first. The words 'Land Registry & Deeds - The Merry Theatre' were scribbled on the front in his Dad's handwriting and Jackson flicked through the pages, seeing that they were full of words that he didn't understand but it seemed to be evidence of his Mum and Dad's ownership of the theatre. He spread the newspaper clippings out on the desk. The black print and pictures had faded to a sepia brown. Jackson stared at the top headline. 'Merry Theatre Causes Family Feud'.

"Billy Merry this week confirmed that the Merry Theatre is under new management as his grandson, Albert Merry, steps into the role with immediate effect. Mr Merry confirmed that the theatre will no longer be managed by his son, Charlie, due to his ill health. Albert Merry commented, "I am honoured to be stepping into my grandfather's and father's shoes. The Merry Theatre is an institution and I promise that my wife Martha and I will commit ourselves wholeheartedly to its continued success."

It is understood that Charlie Merry's sister, Annabel McCreedy, wife of notorious bank robber, Ernest McCreedy had filed legal action against the decision before it was announced, stating, "The Merry Theatre should rightfully be passed to my family as I am Charlie's sibling. My sons, Augustus and Walter, have a right to their inheritance." Ms McCreedy's appeal has since been rejected by the Court."

Jackson stared at the pictures next to the article. One of his great-grandfather standing proudly with his hand on Albert's shoulder. His Dad looked young and his eyes twinkled even through the sepia. The second picture was of his Great Aunt Annabel standing with her husband Ernest and their two sons. All four with miserable expressions. Jackson peered more closely at the young men. One larger with hair pulled across his head like string. The other slim and weaselly, a sly look in his eye. It was them! The men from across the road. From the Grand Theatre. It was THEM! The string-haired man and the

Weasel were the McCreedys, his Dad's cousins! Everything suddenly fell into place. They thought the Merry was *theirs*. They had set out to ruin his parents by setting up a rival theatre directly across the road. They had been the ones vandalising the Merry, stealing money, poaching actors, making it look like Albert was guilty of hurting George. It was THEM!

Jackson's hands started to shake as he held the paper. Suddenly, there was a noise. A heavy clunk and click and Jackson realised it was the stage door of the theatre opening. He crouched down behind the desk. The footsteps were hurried. And they belonged to more than one person.

"I'm so sorry, I've looked everywhere in the house, even in the kitchen cupboards! I've called round every friend I could think of. I'm so sorry. The Sergeant's boss wouldn't let me see you until I agreed to guarantee your bail! And then I couldn't get the money until this morning…"

Jackson listened carefully. As the voice got closer, he realised it was Seamus and he was flinging the doors of each room open as he strode down the corridor. The doors slammed against walls and echoed around the empty theatre. But who was the other person with him? Jackson curled up as small as he could under the desk. He didn't want to be found and taken somewhere away from the theatre. He couldn't be. He still had to find the box.

"Jackson!" Seamus shouted. "Jackson! Are you in here?"

"No," Jackson mouthed silently.

"Jackson?" shouted another voice.

He froze and strained his ears to listen more carefully. "Jackson, please!" It was his Mum! "Where are you?" she cried out.

"We'll find him Martha, he won't have gone far," Seamus said calmly. "And Albert will be out on bail too this afternoon, I've made sure of that. Ridiculous business."

Jackson started to move, he wanted to go to his Mum, to have a huge hug and to tell her all about his Dad's cousins, about the box and his magical friends. Everything. But something stopped him. Would she listen to him? Would she understand? Would she believe him? She would stop him from trying to find the box, he knew it. Thinking quickly, he grabbed a pencil from the desk and scribbled on the newspaper clipping, '*It was them. They own the Grand. I'll be there tonight, love Jackson x.*'

Now he needed to make his exit. Quickly he turned to the sash window and slid it open as quietly as he could. Then he clambered out, but stopped as he looked at the long drop. He realised he hadn't *quite* thought this through. He heard the office door open and his Mum's voice say, "Jackson?"

He had no choice, he let go and landed in a heap in the bushes below. His hands and legs stung with scrapes and scratches but he knew he had to disappear quickly and hoped his Mum would see his note and understand his hastily scribbled message. He ran along by the side of the wall, trampling over shrubs and stones and round into the courtyard. He needed to get into the Grand and he didn't have long to wait until the doors would be open.

CHAPTER TWENTY-FIVE

In the dark depths of the Grand Theatre, the Weasel was watching as McCreedy rubbed his sticky hands gleefully and cracked his knuckles with a cringeworthy click. The two men looked disturbingly pleased with themselves.

"Seems our dear cousin and his wife are finally getting their comeuppance," McCreedy scoffed as he clamped his hand down on top of the props box that sat in the centre of his desk. "So this is *the* box."

"Even *you* might be impressed with this," the Weasel said, sounding rather arrogant.

McCreedy pulled the box towards him and fumbled with the clasp, his hands clattering against the metal impatiently. "How does the blasted thing work?" he snapped, pushing the box towards his brother.

The Weasel pulled the box roughly across the desk towards him and span it around to face him. He flicked open the clasp and lifted the lid with one easy movement. Then turned the box back to face his brother, trying to contain his irritation. McCreedy stared greedily into the box, reaching a clammy hand towards the props. He grabbed at the lamp and as he clumsily pulled it out of the box, there was tentative knock at the door. The Weasel turned angrily towards the sound and

166

just as he did... Ting! The Genie appeared behind McCreedy, blinking, a little startled. He immediately recognised the man in front of him, even from the back of his head and ducked down behind the man's chair, trying to hold his breath.

"Yes?" he heard the Weasel demand as McCreedy slammed the lid of the box shut, still clutching the lamp in his hand. Emma stood nervously in the doorway amidst a mountain of mauve material.

"Well, step forward, girl. Don't loiter in the corridor," McCreedy ordered.

Emma turned sideways to get through the door and held the dress in her hands as best she could as the two men stared at her. She was quickly starting to realise that she didn't much like her new bosses. She hadn't wanted to leave her role at the Merry Theatre but the job of lead costume designer at the Grand had been too good to refuse. It was definitely a step up for her career but these brothers were very strange. Firstly, they had sworn her to secrecy about taking the job and secondly, they seemed to be just plain mean. Albert and Martha had always been so kind, so sweet. She had heard the town gossip about them being arrested... How terrible, how... Her thoughts were interrupted by her new boss' voice.

"Well?"

"I thought I should show you the finished product before I show it to Miss Warblerina," she smiled. "Is it what you..."

"How would I know? That's what we employed *you* for!" McCreedy roared stopping Emma mid-sentence and rising to his feet. "Out, out!"

She stumbled backwards, partly under the weight of the dress and partly in shock.

"Miss Warblerina asked for you to approve the dress and her

room before she arrives so we don't waste… I mean, *take* her time and…" she mumbled.

McCreedy's tone immediately changed. "Well! Why didn't you say so, girl! Take the dress to her dressing room immediately. We must ensure everything is in place for our star!"

As he rose to his feet and with the Weasel still glaring at Emma, the Genie took his chance, crawling as quickly as he could behind the wingback armchair in the corner of the room. Emma cowered and lowered her eyes, only then spotting the child moving in the background. She looked at him, bewildered. McCreedy was picking up the box and opening the cupboard beneath his desk. Emma's eyes darted to the box. It looked like a small treasure chest, wooden and worn and there were some words on the side that looked like they had been burnt into the wood.

"The Merry Players," she read silently as the box disappeared into the cupboard and McCreedy threw the lamp in on top of it. The Weasel scowled and took a menacing step towards her as McCreedy locked the cupboard door and placed the key in his pocket. He barrelled towards Emma and she had no choice but to bundle herself and the dress through the doorframe.

The Weasel glanced back into the room and hissed, "You can wait." He slinked out into the corridor, closing the door behind him. The Genie leant back, his heart beating fiercely. He realised he was leaning against a board or a plank of wood maybe. Curiously, he lifted the corner of the sheet that was covering it and immediately recognised the paintwork. It was the Merry Theatre sign. And behind it Billy and Constance's portrait. Seeing their friendly faces, he knew what he had to do.

Meanwhile, Jackson was unsure where to hide. He had to get out of the street and into the Grand. The whole town knew about his parents' arrest. And they knew his face. They would all want to ask questions if he was spotted. He pulled his collar up as high as he could and stepped into the alleyway next to the Grand. His stomach rumbled loudly. He felt light-headed. What would the Genie do? What would the Fairy Godmother do? He felt a stab of sadness as he thought about his friends. What if he never saw them again? He couldn't afford to think about that now. He needed to come up with a plan to expose his Dad's cousins. Jackson thought for a moment about what the Genie had said to him on that very first night.

"... of course, they have to use a little imagination..."

What would his friends do? The Prince wouldn't let anything get in his way. He would run at the doors of the Grand to get in. The Fairy Godmother would use her kindness. Puck would use her playfulness. Beauty would use her logic and creativity. And the Genie, well, he would use his cheekiness and his self-belief. He would just be certain that he could fix things. He would use his very own brand of magic.

"Cakeshoes," Jackson whispered under his breath to gather his courage as he stepped out into the street and headed straight towards the doors.

The Genie had waited behind the chair for a while to make sure the coast was clear and was now grappling with the cupboard, trying to prize it open. It wouldn't budge.

"Don't worry, I'll get Jackson!" he whispered through the wood, imagining his friends could somehow hear him. He tiptoed over to the door and leant against it to see if he could hear anyone outside. Nothing. He opened it cautiously and peered out. Was it his imagination or was there a chill in the air? He was just in time to see McCreedy and the Weasel disappear into a room at the far end of the corridor, with Emma in tow carrying a dark suit. He could hear the orchestra gathering, chattering and preparing to take their places to warm up. Now was his only chance to get out of the office and so he took it, like a mouse scurrying along the hallway, unsure which way he should go to escape.

Outside, a busy man in an apron was cleaning the Grand doors. He looked with surprise at the boy who had suddenly appeared and paused his polishing for a moment.

"The boss is expecting me," Jackson blurted out, using his grown up voice in an effort to disguise himself. "I've got the... the... um... cufflinks for Harry Cuthbert."

Jackson looked the man straight in the eyes, determined not to waver. There was silence for a moment as the cleaner looked at him suspiciously. "Cufflinks? Well, where are they?"

Jackson's eyes flickered. He could feel his breath quickening. Heat was creeping up his face. "BUBBLEPUMPKIN," he imagined the Fairy Godmother saying to him.

"I'd rather not open the box outside actually," Jackson said, surprising himself with his defiant tone. "They're very expensive. I don't want anyone seeing them." He was happy with his story. He could imagine the Genie saying the same thing.

The cleaner turned back towards the door and continued to polish the handles. "On your bike, you rascal. I wasn't born yesterday. It's more likely you've got your eye on something you want to nick rather than something to give the boss."

Jackson looked at the back of the man's head, more and more

aware that he was out in the open and anyone could spot him at any time. The cleaner spun round, his expression suddenly more aggressive.

"I said, get out of here!" he snapped and Jackson turned around, scuttling away. What now?

Inside, the Genie heard footsteps in the corridor. He looked around him for the nearest door to hide behind, not realising that it was the door to Miss Warblerina's dressing room. He closed the door behind him as quietly as he could. The room was as opulent as the star herself. Her demands had all been met to secure her booking. There were multi-coloured sweets in glass jars, with all the yellow jelly ones removed at her request and all manner of lotions and perfumes lined up on an antique dressing table. A huge pile of necklaces and bracelets were strewn across the surface, a glittering array for Serena to choose from. And a full length, silver framed mirror polished by Emma until it was gleaming, stood in one corner. In the opposite corner the diva's magnificent dress hung on a rail, its skirts so long and multi-layered, they trailed across the floor. It was perfect to hide behind and the Genie dashed over, just in time to hear the door open as the Weasel peered inside. The Genie crouched down, listening carefully.

"She won't miss one now will she?" the Weasel sneered to himself and there was a jangling sound as he lifted one of the necklaces and let it fall into his inside pocket. Then he turned on his heel and closed the door sharply behind him, leaving the Genie to peer out from behind the dress desperate to make his escape.

CHAPTER TWENTY-SIX

Outside the Grand Theatre, the hubbub was growing with curious onlookers starting to mill around.

"Sort it out. Now!" the Weasel seethed through his teeth as he stood staring at the most minuscule mark on the red carpet that led from the door of the Grand to the kerb. The cleaner, who had seemed so confident earlier, cowered on the carpet scrubbing the dot of dirt.

"Get out of the way!" McCreedy hissed to his brother and the cleaner as he spotted Micky Taleteller approaching. "People don't want to be greeted by the sight of you two!" He glared aggressively and the cleaner scuttled away while the Weasel stared at him.

"Welcome! Welcome!" he said, changing his tone. He extended his hand and it stuck to Micky's palm like cold, wet, dough.

"Mr McCreedy, pleasure to be here. Wouldn't miss a newsworthy night like this for the world!"

"Wise man. Now, there's a prime position for you just here behind the ropes."

Micky found himself being ushered to a spot next to the entrance, alongside several other clamouring journalists who shuffled unhappily as McCreedy positioned his new favourite.

"I'll be *expecting* front page for this, of course," he growled glaring at Micky. A shiver shot down Micky's spine and he swore he could have heard, "Or you'll be sorry."

McCreedy grimaced at him and turned away. Maybe he'd misheard.

Jackson wasn't sure how long he'd been in the cold alleyway. The ground was wet so he had been pacing up and down trying to keep warm. His stomach rumbled. Every now and then he edged along the wall and peered around the corner. Not at the front of the building, he'd given up on that after being challenged by the cleaner. Now he was at the back of the building. It occurred to him that the Grand Theatre must have a stage door just like the Merry. And he was right. The street parallel to the theatre's entrance was narrow and mainly residential. Houses built of dark stone stood in uniform rows with large sash windows looking out on the back of the new theatre. There was no sign over the stage door yet but it was obvious that's what it was as people had been arriving for the past couple of hours, carrying all manner of instruments. The Grand orchestra, readying themselves for their first performance. Jackson pulled the collars of his jacket around his face and observed. Sooner or later, surely someone would leave the door ajar. But every time he heard the door open, he would hear the clunk-click of it locking heavily behind the person who had entered. That was until now. As he peered around the corner, he could see the door was at a slight angle. Not quite closed. The street lights hadn't come on yet and in the dusky gloom, he could see a sliver of light emanating from inside. It was now or never.

Jackson kept his head down, watching his feet as they paced towards the door. If he gave it a second's thought, he knew he wouldn't do it so he pushed any thought of panic from his mind, thinking only of his parents and how he had to clear their names. The door was heavy as he pulled at it and slipped inside. He glanced around, trying to get his bearings. To his left, a little way down the corridor, a man he didn't recognise who had his back to him. He was deep in conversation with a lady who was carrying a bunch of flowers almost as big as herself. To Jackson's right, a wall, a dead end. But in front of him, a doorway with a velvet curtain across it. Quickly Jackson tucked himself behind the curtain and as he did so, he stumbled backwards. He realised there was no ground beneath his foot and felt himself twist and fall, his arms flailing, grabbing at the first thing he could. A railing. His knee hit a surface, his hand gripped the bannister. His shoulder felt like his arm had been pulled out. It took him a moment to pull himself together.

"Who would put stairs behind a curtain?" he thought angrily.

Suddenly he could hear a voice bellowing on the other side of the velvet.

"Make sure those flowers are in Serena's dressing room before she arrives. And take the carnations out, she can't bear carnations. They'll be trouble if she finds them in there."

Jackson quickly scuttled down the stairs away from the voice, just in time to hear a thundering of feet through the ceiling above him. And in the cluttered space below, he realised, he was underneath the stage.

At the front of the Grand, the lights in the usually dim street were dazzling. Harry was feeling anxious. He wanted to be inside warming up his voice but his new boss had insisted that he joined him in the cold. He could just see through the gathering crowd across the road to the darkness of the Merry Theatre and he felt his heart sink. He couldn't believe what he had heard about Albert and Martha. His thoughts stopped as McCreedy plonked a heavy arm around his shoulders.

"Ladies and gentlemen! Members of the press! May I introduce you to the, well, the *male* star of our show, Mr Harry Cuthbert."

With that he started to clap his hands together like a seal. The crowd copied, clapping and nodding in approval. Harry looked at the faces that now gazed at him. On one side, a group of theatre-goers, the audience for the night, eager to enter the auditorium but even more eager to catch a close up glimpse of the stars of the show. And on the other side, a throng of journalists staring at him, pointing cameras and flashbulbs in his direction. Their quick fire lights briefly blinding him as he attempted to smile and to imitate the movie stars he had seen in newspapers. All the while conscious that they could probably see his nerves jangling.

With his new boss planting the palm of his hand firmly on his back, Harry found himself being pushed towards the journalists.

"Micky Taleteller, Sunday Chronicle," the first and seemingly loudest journalist shouted, accosting Harry. "Tell me, how did you feel when you first found out you would be singing with Serena Warblerina?"

"Well, I was thrilled, of course," Harry replied honestly as the journalists started scribbling furiously in their notebooks. "I mean, me, Harry Cuthbert, singing with a national treasure! I still can't believe it!"

"You'd better believe it, it's happening in less than an hour!" Micky teased. "And what was Miss Warblerina like when you first met her?"

Harry had actually found her to be rather over the top. Unlike anyone he had ever worked with at the Merry Theatre. But he thought best not to tell anyone that so he said, "Oh charming, utterly charming. And, as you know, she has the voice of an angel."

Right on cue, there was a sudden clattering of horses' hooves and the rattling sound of carriage wheels on the cobbles. *She* had arrived. The *real* star of the show, arriving in her own inimitable, extravagant style. Suddenly Harry was all but forgotten as everyone clamoured to watch as the carriage came to a stop in line with the red carpet. A footman jumped down to open the door of the carriage, revealing the biggest cloud of taffeta and lace that any of the crowd had ever seen. McCreedy rushed over and turned to glare at Harry who realised that, he too, should be rushing. With rather a lot of rustling the mountain of material started to move and Miss Serena Warblerina finally emerged, smiling a radiant smile at her adoring fans. Her trademark trio of scarves winding around and around her neck and shoulders, all the way up to her ears. She wasn't wearing a hat, all too aware that the press would want to see her face and photograph her, so her hair was braided and curled and twisted and twirled into a huge and extravagant style, adorned with real flowers and sparking jewels for good measure. McCreedy took her hand and bowed as low down as he could. Which wasn't particularly low. Harry also bowed simply because, well, he wasn't sure what else to do.

"Miss Warblerina!" the press shouted. "Serena! Over here!" And at the same time the crowd called, "Can I have your autograph, Miss?"

The star looked at them all graciously as she floated along and, as she did, the footman slammed the carriage door shut.

As Serena moved towards her adoring fans, the journalists still clamouring for her attention, it was Harry who spotted it first. The end of one of Miss Warblerina's scarves clamped firmly in the carriage door. The coachman was about to pull away. The horses slowly started to move forwards. The scarf stretched as it was being pulled tighter and tighter.

"Stop!" Harry suddenly shouted. "STOP!" But it was impossible for the coachman to hear him above the hubbub. Harry thought quickly, grabbing his co-star by both shoulders, he started spinning her. Twirling Miss Warblerina round and round like a spinning top until all of her scarves had unravelled, two falling to the floor and the third flying away down the street with the carriage, off into the night. Cameras flashed, ladies shrieked, men gasped and McCreedy looked on with utter fury. Miss Warblerina's look of shock erupted into anger as she watched the carriage disappear and realised what had just happened. She put her hands up to cover her exposed neck and throat.

"Get me inside, this instant! My voice will be ruined!" she hissed at Harry and they rustled along the red carpet as fast as they could with mounds of material in their wake, leaving McCreedy to deal with the baying crowd.

CHAPTER TWENTY-SEVEN

Soon, the Grand audience were settling into their luxurious seats marvelling at the grandeur of the dress circle floating above them. The glittering gilt edges of the enormous stage twinkled in the light of the chandelier. The press, who had been given some of the best seats in the house, were poised only a few rows from the front, ready to note everything for their reviews. The *best* seat in the house was reserved for the Lady Mayoress, Victoria Strudwick who was parading down the centre aisle in an extravagant hat, courting attention from all sides. The townsfolk shouted greetings as she drifted by and Mr Greengold, who she had insisted attend with her, sidled along beside her, not at all used to being in the limelight. They took their seats just as the lights lowered. A hush descended. The show was about to begin.

McCreedy, puffed up with pompous pride, was standing with his brother and their stars in the wings. Serena distanced herself from them, making her superiority quite obvious as Emma straightened the hem of her dress. Harry could hear his heartbeat booming in his ears as he tried to control his nerves. If any one of them had turned their head, they would have seen a small boy tiptoe past behind them unnoticed, his face screwed up in concentration. The Genie, desperate to escape. He had been trapped in Harry's dressing room for the past half an hour, crouching underneath the dressing table, hidden by the tablecloth. He had managed to escape Serena's room only to be stopped in his tracks by her arrival and then narrowly missing Harry as he went into his dressing room, muttering about how ridiculous his co-star was. But now the Genie took his chance and with the orchestra in the pit, the stars waiting in the wings and all eyes on the imminent performance, he would finally be able to find his way out to find Jackson.

Or so he thought. Suddenly the Weasel stalked back out into the corridor. Quick! The Genie pinned himself to the alcove of the nearest doorway. Then, needing to get out of sight, he ducked behind the velvet curtain by the stage door and ran down the stairs behind it. The cluttered space below the stage was dark and full of shadows. His eyes slowly adjusted to what little light there was. He could hear a single set of footsteps walking across the stage and he watched as fresh sawdust from the newly laid floorboards drifted gently from the ceiling above his head, sparkling like glitter. As the Genie peered upwards, listening out for the performance to begin, he heard a whisper.

"It *IS* you!"

From the gloom, out stepped a boy. He looked exhausted but his grin shone from ear to ear.

"Jackson!" the Genie exclaimed. "What are you doing under here?"

"Sssshush!" his friend responded, laughing quietly. The boys hugged each other warmly and Jackson felt tears in his eyes. "I can't believe it! You're here! I thought I'd lost you all."

In the foyer, Sergeant Goodman was showing his police badge to allow him and his Merry companions to pass without question. Albert looked around him. It felt as though his life was in tatters. Not only had he and Martha spent the night in prison, not only did they have to be bailed out but when they finally got home, they had discovered that their son was missing! They had tried to take comfort from Jackson's note but none of it made any sense. Did his cousins really own the Grand? Did they really have that much of a vendetta against him that they would build an entire theatre to get back at him and his grandfather?

Albert and Martha couldn't believe their eyes. The Grand's opulence was beyond compare. The gold of the doors shimmered so brightly and their feet sank so deeply into the carpet that Albert suddenly felt quite woozy. He held on to Martha to steady himself. The group made their way into the auditorium, shuffling their way along the back wall as the lights dimmed. They watched as the curtain slowly rose. A single spotlight shone on the stage, creating a perfect circle of light on the polished boards. There was a hush as the audience waited, holding their breath, not wanting to shatter the silence. And then the violins began, then the cellos, then the flutes and music filled the theatre as Harry stepped forward into the light, trying to disguise the fact that he was shaking from head to toe. Then, taking a deep gulp of air into his lungs he began to sing and a sense of calm spread through him. The audience, many of whom had seen Harry act numerous times at the Merry Theatre, began to edge towards the front of their seats. They were all thinking exactly the same thing, "I didn't know he could sing so well."

Albert smiled despite himself and squeezed Martha's hand. Now he understood. Harry, his protégé, simply wanted to sing, that was why he had left. He hadn't betrayed him. He had just needed his voice to be heard.

"He's got some voice on him, that's for sure," Martha whispered to Albert and all Albert could do was nod.

Under the stage, as Harry's voice soaked through the floorboards, the boys chattered in whispers. The Genie looked at Jackson intensely as he shared what he knew. "They took the box. It's locked up in their office. I'm only here because they forgot to put the lamp back in," he garbled quickly.

"They're the reason my Mum and Dad got arrested!" Jackson exclaimed.

"What? They're in prison?"

"They've been stealing from us for months. I've figured it all out. All the vandalism, things going missing, George being hurt, us losing money. It was all them."

"Yes! The Merry sign! And your great-grandparents' portrait! They're hidden in their office," the Genie said, almost excited that all the pieces of the puzzle were coming together.

"That's the proof we need!" Jackson stated triumphantly.

"But why would they do it all? Just because they don't want the competition?" Genie asked.

"They're my Dad's cousins. Their mother thought the Merry should have been given to her and they've made it their mission to close us down. And they've managed it! My Mum and Dad haven't done anything wrong! We've got to help them and tell everyone the truth."

Harry's song was coming to a close and as he sang out one final wonderful note, the audience were on their feet, applauding wildly. Harry took a step back, astounded.

"Thank you so much, ladies and gentlemen. Thank you," he could feel his voice cracking with emotion and cleared his throat to compose himself. "And now, it is my great pleasure to introduce you to a true legend of our lifetime and the star of our show, Miss Serena Warblerina."

He flung his right arm out to one side and as the audience started to clap ecstatically, Serena swept out onto the stage, slightly hampered by the weight of the magnificent dress that Emma had created for her. Several more spotlights suddenly flickered into life and Miss Warblerina was bathed in their dazzling glow. She looked out at her adoring fans, taking Harry's hand and dropping into a sudden and dramatic curtsy, sitting down on the folds of her skirts as if they were a nest around her. Harry felt altogether uncomfortable as Serena rose and dropped his hand abruptly, as if to signal that his moment had passed. He took the hint, leaving the stage and leaving her to her first solo.

The audience once again fell silent, waiting for the diva to sing as beautifully as they had been told that she could. The orchestra started up. Her cue came and Miss Warblerina opened her mouth. And... Nothing. Even Serena herself looked a little shocked. Her face crumpled in confusion. The conductor looked up from the orchestra pit quizzically and guided the musicians into repeating a couple of bars to give Serena another chance to start the song. Her jaw lowered, her mouth widened, the moment came... And went. This time Serena's hand shot to her throat in panic.

"My voice!" she mouthed but no sound came out. She

looked around indignantly, trying to sing. The audience shifted in their seats, unsure what was happening. The Weasel and McCreedy stood with Harry in the wings watching aghast.

"What on earth is going on?" McCreedy demanded angrily. "Is this your fault, man?" He looked at Harry accusingly.

"No, no, I don't think so. I think she's lost her voice," Harry stammered.

"Well, I. Can. See. That! Don't just stand there you idiot, get on that stage and sing!"

"But, how do I…" Harry was about to ask how he should ask Serena to leave the stage but McCreedy's hand was once again on his back, pushing him into position. Finding himself in the light of the stage, he attempted an apologetic expression and held his hand out to Serena. But rather than go graciously, she had other ideas and lifting her skirts slightly, she stamped her tiny little foot furiously, scowled at him and stormed off. Harry did the only thing he could think to do and began to sing, picking up the song effortlessly to be greeted by a wave of applause from the audience. As Serena stomped dramatically past the two men, McCreedy glared at his brother and signalled that he should follow him into the corridor.

Jackson and the Genie had crept up the stairs and were about to pull the velvet curtain back when they heard the two men.

"Well? What are YOU going to do about THIS? We can't have a whole show of just *him singing*. Think. Of. Something." McCreedy hissed.

"Stop panicking," the Weasel said under his breath. "We have the magic box. We'll simply reveal its tricks. The audience won't believe their eyes. Now *that* will be a headline."

Behind the curtain, the Genie and Jackson stared at each

183

other wide-eyed. McCreedy looked at his brother incredulously, his eyebrows so high on his face that it looked like they may crawl off over his head. He lowered his voice to a growl.

"We are in the MIDDLE of a show! Whatever it can or cannot do, I don't see how our star can be replaced with a box!" Even as he spoke, the man's mind was cast back to the Merry boy's friend who had disappeared from his hands. He shook his head.

"We need an *ACT*," he growled as he continued. "Our debut show is FALLING TO PIECES!"

"You don't think children appearing from a magic box will astonish our audience and leave them wanting more?" the Weasel said confidently. "It will establish us as the best theatre in town. Well, have YOU got a better idea?" He stared at his brother. "I thought not."

McCreedy didn't have a better idea. Looking like he was fit to explode, he threw his keys at his brother angrily and stormed away towards Serena's dressing room. And as the Weasel scurried down the corridor, the boys knew they had to stop him. But how?

CHAPTER TWENTY-EIGHT

On stage, Harry was breaking into his third song. One that had been planned as a duet but he now found himself singing both parts. He couldn't help but notice the eyes of the audience members flicking towards the wings every now and then, clearly wondering what had happened to the star of the show. McCreedy, having been told in no uncertain terms by Serena that she wanted to be left alone, stood seething backstage. The Weasel meanwhile, was in the office, grabbing the Merry Players' treasure chest from the cupboard.

Jackson was pacing in the small space under the stage. The Genie stood with his hand on his chin, looking upwards, thinking.

"He's going to take the box on stage," he whispered. "He'll open it, tip out the props and everyone will appear and he'll claim the magic as his own! And more importantly, he'll have control over when we can all get home. Or even, *whether* we can get home."

"Come on! We'll confront them! They're thieves! I'm not scared of them!" Jackson announced as he headed towards the stairs. As he grabbed the bannister, he noticed his hand was shaking.

For once, the Genie was glued to the spot. "I don't know. I've been attacked by McCreedy before."

Jackson turned to look back at his friend desperately and as he did, he noticed the lines of light shining through the floorboards above him. Suddenly he realised what it was. A trapdoor! From the stage, to the space they were standing in. On the floor below, a pile of mattresses to cushion anyone who fell through it.

"I know how to stop him!" Jackson announced and as he spoke, just a few feet away in the office upstairs, the Weasel opened the lid of the box and threw the lamp back inside. "We can use the trap..."

The Genie vanished. And Jackson knew immediately what had happened. "... Door," he whispered finishing his sentence and staring up at the square of light.

As Serena Warblerina snatched a honey and lemon concoction angrily from Emma, Harry continued to sing the songs that should have been hers and the crowd remained unsettled. The Weasel curled his hands around the box and carried it out into the corridor where McCreedy was storming towards him.

"Well?" he demanded, spitting with anger. "We can't have that Cuthbert man on forever. Our audience are expecting A SPECTACULAR SPECTACLE!"

"And I have it right here," the Weasel said in a sinister tone as he made his way towards the wing. "I'll go on stage after this song."

"You WILL NOT!" McCreedy fumed. "I will go on!" He tried to grab the box but the Weasel refused to let go. Harry sang out his last note and was once again met with rapturous applause. He glanced across to the wing to see the two men arguing and then McCreedy pushing his brother to one side and stepping confidently out into the spotlight. The Weasel following closely behind.

"Our new talent, singing sensational sensation Harry Cuthbert!" McCreedy said, holding one arm out towards Harry. Harry took his bow as the man sidled uncomfortably close to him and said two words through the gritted teeth of his fake smile, "Get OFF."

Harry immediately left the stage utterly confused about what he was meant to do next. He watched from the wing, waiting to be beckoned back on.

Albert and Martha stood at the back of the theatre in the shadows, staring at the men who had just appeared on stage. Even in the darkness, Martha could see the colour drain from Albert's cheeks as he squinted. Then squinted some more. Then raised his eyebrows and slowly whispered.

"They're my cousins. It's Augustus and Walter. Just as Jackson said. My goodness. It *is* them!" Albert gasped and turned to Sergeant Goodman. "And that's Jackson's box! I don't know how they've got it but that box isn't theirs. It's the Merry Players box."

"Albert, are you saying those men have stolen goods?" the Sergeant whispered gruffly.

"YES! But I don't care about that. Where's Jackson? I need to find our son!" With that he started off towards the front of the auditorium. By now the back rows of the audience were looking around to see what the kerfuffle was about.

"It's Martha Merry!" "Isn't that Albert?" They could hear their voices as they strode past with Sergeant Goodman close behind.

McCreedy looked out at the audience and boomed, "Ladies and gentlemen, while our star Serena Warblerina warms her voice up a little more for her performance, we have another SPECTACULAR spontaneous treat in store. Something really special. My business partner and brother, has an amazing, ASTONISHING, magic trick. You just won't be able to believe your eyes!"

The audience were restless. Weren't they here to see a superstar performing? Not a small-time magician.

"Ladies and gentlemen, Lady Mayoress, I give you Walter McCreedy…" McCreedy continued, revelling in his new role as ringmaster.

The Weasel looked out at the crowd. This was it. He held the box firmly in both hands, being careful to keep the side that read *The Merry Players* close to his chest. "All I need is this… little… box… At first glance, it looks like it is just a box… But watch… very… VERY… closely…"

All eyes gazed up at him, waiting for something to happen. Suddenly there was a creaking sound. And then another creak. McCreedy looked down at his feet with alarm. And just as the Weasel realised where the sound was coming from. BANG! WHOOSH! The trapdoor beneath their feet gave way and swung open and down the brothers fell. Ten feet down. CRASH! Into a heap of limbs, sprawled on the pile of mattresses below. The audience gasped all at once. A man in the front row let out a shocked scream. Was this the magic trick? A couple in the second row started to giggle nervously and then the noise started to spread as more and more people started to laugh in shock and amusement.

The Weasel landed with a THUD. McCreedy fell heavily on

top of him and as their heads knocked together, the two were momentarily knocked out cold. The box flew out of the Weasel's hands, clattered onto the floor and fell open. Out spilled the ornate lamp, the elaborate crown, the purple silk flower, the sparkling wand and the ruby ring and then... Ting! Ting! Ting! Ting! Ting! The Genie, the Prince, the Fairy Godmother, Beauty and Puck appeared like magic, all around the dazed and confused villains, all a little startled. Jackson jumped down from the table he had been standing on to pull the trapdoor lever. It had worked! He looked around at his friends as they all tried to get their bearings.

"We're in the other theatre. That's why it looks different," Jackson explained.

Beauty looked up at the light that was streaming through the trapdoor, "Is it show time?" she said excitedly, having no idea what was going on. Bemused laughter and chatter from the audience drifted down through the opening.

"Not quite. My parents have been arrested."

"What? Why? When?" Jackson's friends chorused.

"They've been framed by my Dad's cousins, these scoundrels!" Jackson pointed at the men. "They own this theatre. They've been stealing from the Merry for months. Maybe years. And I'm going to expose them. Right now, in front of this whole audience."

The Fairy Godmother stared at the two men as Jackson picked the box up from the floor and frantically looked around for the props. The others bent down to help him as he looped the Prince's crown around his arm. The handle of the Genie's lamp hung on his thumb and he put Beauty's ring on his finger.

"Got it!" the Fairy Godmother exclaimed as she held her wand aloft.

"Me too!" smiled Puck as she twirled her flower between her thumb and forefinger and then shoved it in her pocket.

"Great! Right, Genie! Quickly! I need you to get the Merry Theatre sign from where you saw it and to bring it onto the stage. Take Beauty with you to help!" Jackson ordered. The Genie led the way, racing up the stairs, with Beauty in tow.

"What on earth…" It was the Weasel. He had opened his eyes to find himself pinned to the pile of mattresses by his brother and was turning a deep shade of red with pure rage.

The chatter from the audience was dying down as they waited. Harry stood stunned in the wing, staring at the space where the brothers had been. He could just see the conductor looking up at him from the orchestra pit, raising his eyebrows and hands as if asking a question. Harry pointed at himself and the conductor nodded vigorously. A moment later the orchestra struck up the first chords of the next planned song. Harry took a deep breath and stepped back out into the light, hoping he was about to do the right thing as he started to sing.

"Help me with this!" Jackson pleaded, trying to be heard above the music, as he grabbed at a ladder that was leaning against the wall of the basement. "I need to get onto the stage."

"The stage?" the Fairy Godmother asked as she ran over to help him. Jackson glanced at her and gulped, white with fear.

"Don't say it!" Jackson said, as they dragged the ladder over until they were level with the trapdoor and leant the top rungs against the floorboards.

"I was just going to say, cakeshoes," the Fairy Godmother said quietly with a twinkle in her eye. "Go!"

"Get off me!" the Weasel suddenly shouted. As Jackson

started to climb, the Weasel pushed at his brother, wriggling and squirming as he tried to free himself. McCreedy made a grumbling sound and rolled further onto the Weasel's chest, pinning him even more awkwardly than before. The Prince and Puck positioned themselves next to the men, the Prince bravely brandishing his sword.

"You stay where you are! Or I'll…"

"You'll what, boy?" the Weasel sneered finally freeing himself and rising onto his feet until he stood looking down his nose at the Prince.

"I'll fight you!" the Prince continued, bravely. The Weasel swiped at him, snatched his sword effortlessly and callously snapped it in two. That was it. The Prince saw red. He ran at the Weasel and aimed straight for his stomach, punching with both fists. The Weasel held his hand out and pushed it against the Prince's forehead, holding him at arms length, watching him thrash his arms around. Puck, seeing her chance for some mischief, nimbly jumped up on the Weasel's back, putting her hands over his eyes, as the Prince grabbed at his other hand and the three of them wobbled and span towards the stairs.

McCreedy slowly opened his eyes. His face was squashed against the top mattress. "Where am I?" he started and then stopped as he caught sight of Jackson on the ladder. Framed by the square of light that streamed in through the trapdoor, he rose up on his hands and knees menacingly. His eyes darted from one child to another as Jackson and the Fairy Godmother stared back at him and then his gaze settled on the box.

"I see…" he growled as he slowly got to his feet. Jackson looked up and stared his enemy in the eye. "I don't think so, you little… What do you think you are doing *ruining* MY show? After that pathetic father of yours has already tried to *ruin* our LIVES!" he ranted as he lumbered towards the ladder and grabbed at Jackson's ankles.

The Fairy Godmother snatched at McCreedy, grabbing his arm, trying to free Jackson so that he could climb further. "Get off him!" she exclaimed as she felt McCreedy's rubbery hand clamp over her mouth.

"Let go of her, you bully!" Jackson puffed as he kicked against McCreedy's grip. "You framed my Mum and Dad! It's not their fault my great-grandad wanted them to have the Merry!"

"What did you say, boy? It was OURS. It was always meant to be ours." Jackson saw the fury in his Dad's cousin's eyes. "Why should he have all the success with it? Making money, getting all the attention. Being so *NICE* all the time. It's taken us YEARS to get our revenge. YEARS. And now YOU try to ruin our opening night?"

Jackson was breathless. "But he... He didn't... We didn't..."

The Fairy Godmother, watching in horror and unable to speak, couldn't help herself. She kicked the horrid man in the shins with her pointy-toed shoes, making him wince. McCreedy attempted to kick back, almost toppling in the process.

"A little help here, Walter? These irritating *children* are trying to ruin our show!" McCreedy barked at his brother.

The Weasel had managed to pull one of Puck's hands from his face and glared as hard as he could with one eye.

"Don't you get it, Augustus?" he responded. "We can make a fortune from these creatures. They ARE the show!"

The Weasel had managed to twist himself so that he had his arm wrapped around the Prince and he slapped at Puck with his other hand as she snatched at his hair, pulling it up into tufts.

"Will you stop going on about your children's show!" Mc-Creedy seethed. "We have a magnificent star who is *meant* to be on stage RIGHT NOW and these ruffians are trying to disrupt everything! You've always been SUCH a waste of space! You ALWAYS get it WRONG!"

"You wouldn't have been able to do ANY of this without ME! You ungrateful fool!"

Jackson looked between the two men as they spat insults at each other. For the briefest moment, McCreedy let his grip loosen. Jackson took his chance and shook his leg more forcefully than before, managing to free himself.

"Oh NO you DON'T!" the man boomed and his voice carried up and out of the trapdoor onto the stage. Suddenly there was a pause in Harry's singing. The orchestra continued and he picked up the melody again.

"You are not going on that stage," McCreedy hissed under his breath, letting go of the Fairy Godmother and using both hands to pull Jackson by his ankles. Jackson stumbled. Then fell, then tumbled, off the ladder, down onto the floor, sending the crown and lamp spinning across the room. McCreedy didn't look back. He stepped over Jackson, onto the bottom rung and began to climb.

Puck jumped down from the Weasel and grabbed the crown and lamp. As Jackson struggled up from the floor, the Weasel saw his chance and releasing his grip on the Prince, snatched the box from Jackson.

"I think I'll have that, thank you very much boy," he said slowly. "Don't come close to me or I will smash this box in to a thousand pieces."

Jackson froze.

"He doesn't mean it. He wouldn't be able to do that," the Fairy Godmother said, panic in her eyes.

"You don't think so?" the Weasel said scornfully, holding the box above his head as if ready to smash it down on his knee.

"Don't. Don't! Stop it!" Jackson pleaded. "What do you want?"

The Weasel lowered the box. "You will put on your play for us. You will say that you've been rehearsing it secretly for our opening night, all this time. You are *family* after all. One final little insult to your Mum and Dad after they've made such fools of us for all these years."

"We're not doing that!" the Prince exclaimed.

"Yes, we're not doing that!" Puck added, her hands on her hips.

The Fairy Godmother looked at Jackson. "If he smashes the box, we can't get…" she said slowly. "Home."

"You don't need to tell me. I know we have no choice," Jackson said quietly with tears in his eyes and the Weasel's face shaped into a scornful smirk.

As Harry sang out the last long note of his song, the audience couldn't help but be distracted by the red face that suddenly appeared through the hole in the stage. Harry looked down to see what the audience were staring at and was rather shocked to see his boss staring up at him, his head and shoulders now visible and a grin plastered on his face as he realised he was in the spotlight. He couldn't turn back now.

The Mayoress, who enjoyed variety shows, burst into peels of laughter. She leant towards Mr Greengold and whispered, "I'm ever so glad I came along this evening but these men really don't have any idea how to put on a show."

Even Mr Greengold couldn't resist letting out a giggle as the man clambered up the final rungs of the ladder and the music came to an end. Harry, unsure where to put himself, watched as McCreedy crawled clumsily out of the trapdoor on his knees and then, ever so awkwardly and ever so slowly stood up.

Under the stage, Jackson led the way solemnly up the stairs with the Prince, Puck and the Fairy Godmother gathered closely behind him in a huddle, as the Weasel breathed down their necks.

"Stop dawdling, come along. Your audience is waiting," he sneered.

The group made their way into the darkness of the Grand wing. Jackson thought about all the times he had hidden in the wing of the Merry Theatre, watching the plays. How had it come to this? The Weasel guarded them closely, holding the box possessively. Jackson looked out onto the stage where McCreedy was addressing the crowd, directing them to give Harry another round of applause. The spotlight was highlighting the stringy hairs that were scraped across his head. Harry took a bow and looked at his boss, wondering what was going to happen next. As he looked across, he spotted Jackson who mouthed at him silently, "Help."

Harry gulped, unsure what Jackson meant, unsure why he was even there, unsure what to do. It was then that Jackson saw them, just in view in the opposite wing, his friends the Genie and Beauty. His heart leapt. They were pushing something heavy, wrapped in cloth, along the floor. The Merry Theatre sign. Jackson looked up at the Weasel. The man's eyes were on McCreedy, watching him closely. If he looked even slightly to the left, he would see the sign.

"We need my friends," Jackson said suddenly. He had to distract him somehow. The Weasel spun round and glared at him. Jackson had his attention, "We need the others too. For the play. We can't do it without them."

"Well. Where. Are. They?" the Weasel hissed. "You're about to go on."

Jackson took a deep breath. "BUBBLEPUMPKIN!" he exclaimed.

The Fairy Godmother knew exactly what that meant. Jackson had found his courage.

"They're up there!" he pointed towards the rafters.

As the Weasel looked up, Jackson lifted his foot and stamped hard. Really hard. Square on the Weasel's foot. The man gasped. It was just enough to distract him. The Fairy Godmother helped, jumping on the Weasel's feet again and his grip on the box loosened. Just enough for Jackson to prize it from his grasp. And as Jackson did so, he turned and stepped purposefully and deliberately, forwards. Out into the light.

"It's the Merry boy," he heard people say. "That's Jackson, isn't it?" "What's he doing?"

Mr Greengold, who had been enjoying a pleasant, if a little unusual, evening's entertainment, suddenly sat up very straight. The Mayoress grinned. And Albert and Martha, by the edge of the stage with Sergeant Goodman, looked up, their mouths open.

"Jackson!" Albert exclaimed.

Tears came to Martha's eyes, "My boy!"

The Weasel stumbled forwards. He looked across the stage and finally, he saw the Genie and Beauty. Jackson heading defiantly towards them. The Weasel stepped out onto the stage, seething and no longer concerned that he was in full view of the town's great and good. McCreedy span round on his heel, his eyes darting from Jackson to his brother, who was now surrounded by the Prince, Puck and the Fairy Godmother who were all starting to shout.

"CAKESHOES! STARRIVER! CATSOCKS! JAMTREE!" they chanted, distracting the Weasel as much as they could.

"My... my..." McCreedy began, clenching his jaw. "My OPENING NIGHT!" he finally roared, stamping his foot furiously. Looking out, he saw the front row of faces, staring at him with stunned expressions. "I mean, OUR opening night... has only just begun!" he stumbled.

Jackson held the box under one arm and grinned at the Genie and Beauty, motioning them on to the stage, using his free hand to help them to push the sign. Harry joined in, pushing the slab of wood forwards.

"Jackson, what on earth is going on?" Harry asked.

"These men framed my parents. This is the proof!"

The Weasel was now storming towards them and jostling awkwardly with the children around him. The Prince, Puck and the Fairy Godmother all leant a hand, half carrying, half pushing the sign, edging it into full view of the crowd.

CHAPTER TWENTY-NINE

It was at this precise moment that Serena Warblerina decided to make her reappearance in the opposite wing, Emma hurrying after her attentively.

"I have never been treated so appallingly!" she wailed, her voice well and truly back in fine form. And then seeing the commotion on the stage, she added, "Why are there *children* on MY stage?"

Emma stared at all the faces wondering the same herself. "I have no idea," she replied truthfully.

"Get away from me!" the Weasel protested.

"Get them off my stage this instant!" McCreedy seethed at his brother.

"Don't you think that is what I am *trying* to do, you idiot! And it is *our* stage!" he argued.

"Now Jackson, now!" Harry exclaimed.

Jackson looked. It was now or never.

"Ladies and gentlemen," he started, his voice shaking. "Ladies and gentlemen, these men are thieves and liars."

The audience were wrapt with attention.

"Now, now, boy, we can't have you saying things like that can we? This isn't a children's story," McCreedy laughed patronisingly.

Jackson continued, determined. "They have been stealing from The Merry Theatre for months and it's time that everyone knew. They've been trying to ruin us because they thought, WRONGLY, that our theatre should have been theirs. They stole money from us. They stole my great-grandparents' portrait. They stole our actors. They tried to hurt George. They even stole our sign."

With a dramatic gesture, Jackson pulled the sheet from the sign to the floor. The gold lettering glinted in the light. The Merry Theatre, it read.

"They tried to ruin my..." He looked down and there they were, his parents smiling up at him, "... Mum and Dad," he finished.

"Well, this is a turn up for the books!" the Mayoress said delightedly from her seat in the stalls. "It appears your instincts were right, Mr Greengold."

"Oh boo hoo!" said the Weasel, screwing his face up ridiculously as he watched the reunion. "Boo hoo! You were never meant to have the Merry Theatre. It was always meant to be ours! We spent years planning all of this! Planning our revenge. YEARS!"

"So you admit it!" Jackson exclaimed.

"Walter!" McCreedy glared at his brother in shock. "I knew you were up to something," he stated, attempting to extract himself from the unfolding situation, in front of their astounded audience. "I will not have villains working in my establishment, even if you are my brother!"

Two things happened at once. First, Serena swept back into the spotlight, unannounced. The second thing, was that Sergeant

Goodman climbed the steps onto the stage.

"I think that's what's known as a confession," he said raising his eyebrows at the Weasel.

McCreedy, eager to regain control, saw his opportunity, "While the Sergeant… Um… Handles this… The star of our show will sing us another song!"

He looked at the conductor impatiently. "Well, what are you waiting for, man? Play on!" he exclaimed. Then turning towards the Weasel, "Get off the stage, you imbecile. Our star is *trying* to perform," he hissed as Serena moved forwards and sang her first piercing note.

Suddenly, the Weasel bolted. Jackson darted in front of him, looking directly into his weaselly eyes. The friends cheered excitedly. The Weasel tried to turn to weave past Jackson and as he did so, he tripped on Serena Warblerina's mountainous dress and the pair both fell to the floor.

"Argh!" she screeched, landing square on top of him.

McCreedy gasped at the sight of his star sprawled on the floor. At the same time, Sergeant Goodman stepped forwards brandishing his police badge over the Weasel, "Walter McCreedy, I am arresting you, in the name of the law, under suspicion of theft, fraud, conspiracy and attempt to do harm. You do not have to say anything but anything you do say will be taken down in evidence and may be used against you."

Serena scrambled to her feet, the pile of hair usually so well placed on her head tumbling down to one side unceremoniously.

"I have never known such a debacle IN MY LIFE!" she screeched, her voice well and truly restored. And with that off she flounced. Unfortunately for her, she hadn't spotted that the trapdoor was still open and both Serena and her skirts fell abruptly through to the mattresses below with a high-pitched squeal.

The Sergeant leant down and handcuffed the Weasel.

"Ha! Finally! You're getting what you deserve!" McCreedy announced, flipping his hair back out of his eyes.

Sergeant Goodman turned to him, once again showing his police badge.

"And I'm arresting you, Augustus McCreedy, in the name of the law, under suspicion of aiding and abetting a thief and of collaborating in conspiracy. You do not have to say anything but anything you do say will be taken down in evidence."

"Well, this is absolutely positively preposterous!" McCreedy protested as the Sergeant squeezed his wrists into handcuffs too.

Albert and Martha made their way onto the stage and Martha put her arms around Jackson.

"Jackson Benjamin Merry, my brave boy," she said proudly and kissed him on the top of his head. Jackson melted into his Mum's arms.

"You've been working this all out for yourself haven't you, Jackson? And I haven't been listening to you. I'm so sorry," Albert hugged his family and ruffled his son's hair. For once Jackson really didn't mind.

McCreedy settled his gaze on Albert, "You! You stole our theatre. It should have been ours!"

Albert turned to his cousin. "Augustus. It was Billy's wish. It was his choice to make. Don't you remember, I tried to include you, to work with you. You didn't want to be a part of it."

Albert spoke softly. The two villains were led from their own stage and Jackson's friends and the amazed audience cheered.

In the middle of the commotion, Harry appeared at Albert's side. "I'm so sorry, I didn't know who they were. They offered me this amazing opportunity of singing with Serena but they swore me to secrecy. I never would have agreed if I'd known they were plotting against you. I know Emma feels the same, they did the same to her. She only ever wanted to be a costume designer."

"Oh Harry," Albert said kindly, "I know you've always wanted to sing. You were magnificent tonight. I'm sorry I haven't given you the opportunity before. Let's see what we can do about that."

The two men smiled warmly at each other, their friendship firmly back on track.

Outside, Micky Taleteller was waiting for his exclusive interviews with the evening's crowd, camera in hand, notebook in his pocket, pen behind his ear. He couldn't believe his eyes when he saw the Sergeant, frog-marching the two men from the building. SNAP! He would definitely be getting the front page now.

Jackson stood on the Grand Theatre stage with his parents and his friends looking out at all the faces. His Dad, ever the obliging host, stepped forwards.

"Well, it's been rather an eventful evening. But it looks like the night ends here." With that he slowly started to walk off the stage. As he turned, there was a tip tap of steps in the aisle and a figure emerged out of the half-light. It was the

Mayoress, smiling warmly. "We can't end the evening here, my dear fellow. We have a whole second act to fill!"

Jackson hesitated for a moment. He stared out at the audience, who were all looking at him. And although he felt his stomach flip, although he felt his cheeks going red, he couldn't explain what he did next.

"We have a play!" he blurted out. "Me and my friends, we have a play. We've been rehearsing."

There were mutterings from the crowd as his Dad stopped in his tracks and turned to his son.

Jackson looked at his friends for encouragement. The Fairy Godmother's eyes were sparkling. The Genie was grinning. The Prince stood with his hands on his hips, ready for action. Beauty and Puck linked arms and nodded in unison. "We could put it on if you like," Jackson continued.

His Mum was open-mouthed, "A play? That sounds wonderful, Jackson!"

His Dad was amazed and simply said, "Yes!"

The Mayoress addressed the crowd, "Well, what do we think? Would we like to see their play?"

There was a chorus of approval. With the variety of the night so far, the audience were excited to see what would happen next.

"Wonderful!" the Mayoress exclaimed, "Let the show go on!"

"The thing is…" Jackson ventured, finding himself feeling braver by the moment. "We prepared the play so we could put it on to save the Merry Theatre. It's not meant to be performed here. We need to be in *our* theatre."

"We are the Merry Players after all," Puck piped up.

"I know it's not as fancy as this one but it's our home," Jackson said softly.

The Mayoress grinned at his determination.

"As it happens, I would like to help to make it just as fancy as this one. I like to think I'm a good judge of character. The very fact that the McCreedys kept this place so hidden from view made me suspicious of them. And The Merry Theatre has always been an institution in this town. I have always admired your dedication to it as a family. I'm going to ask Mr Greengold to draw up an investment agreement first thing in the morning. That's alright, isn't it Mr Greengold?"

Mr Greengold stood up tentatively and said quietly, "Um, yes. It would be a pleasure."

"You will both still be the managers, of course. I know nothing about running a theatre, I just like to be entertained," the Mayoress laughed warmly.

The Merrys looked at the lady in amazement, not quite believing what they were hearing.

The Mayoress grinned. "And after tonight, I expect this place will be up for sale so you may need to manage this for me too. I think the Merry Concert Hall has a certain ring about it, don't you? And your Merry Theatre can remain the magnificent playhouse it has always been."

"Do you really mean it?" Martha asked as she squeezed Albert's hand tightly, tears coming to her eyes.

"Of course, my dear friends," Victoria Strudwick looked up at the Merrys with honest eyes. "Will you at least consider it?"

"Yes! My goodness. Yes!" they all exclaimed and Jackson turned to hug his parents. The audience and children cheered and whooped. The Mayoress, ever the dramatist, made her way up the steps and shook Albert and Martha's hands. Then she turned to Jackson and held out her hand in the direction of the doors.

CHAPTER TWENTY-NINE

"Now! On with the show!" she announced. "Lead the way, Jackson."

It started with a gentle muttering, then a few people clapping, then cheering, then the audience began to stand and repeat cheerfully, "Lead the way, Jackson!"

"Go on son," said his Dad into his ear.

Jackson knew what he had to do. He jumped down from the stage, into the aisle of the auditorium, where his friends gathered around him. And as he walked through the crowd, everyone followed, even Harry, even the orchestra. *Even* Serena Warblerina, who had been persuaded by Emma to join in on the proviso that she should probably become friends with the Merrys as they were, after all, going to be the new owners of the concert hall. Out into the foyer, out into the street, a streaming crowd of people all in their finery, all making their way into the Merry Theatre, all taking their seats and lining the aisles for the first ever performance by the newly formed Merry Players.

CHAPTER THIRTY

Jackson stood behind the curtain, in the middle of the Merry Theatre stage, alone. His friends ready to take their cues from the wings. His heart was beating so loudly he could hear it in his ears. He could feel it in his chest, in his stomach. He thought about running. Perhaps they could put on the play without him? Perhaps they didn't need a narrator after all? He looked across to one side of the stage. Puck was springing up and down on the spot, like a gymnast warming up for a routine, with a big grin on her face. Beauty was beside her, smoothing her hair, the ruby ring glittering on her finger. The Prince stood regally, wearing his crown, still mourning the loss of his sword but bravely soldiering on. Jackson looked to the other side and the Fairy Godmother was reciting her lines, under her breath. Realising he was looking over, she grinned at him and mouthed, "CAKESHOES!"

It was the first word she had shouted on the Merry stage that night when he had first found his confidence and he laughed.

"CAKESHOES!" he mouthed back and she smiled.

Jackson looked across at the Genie, his friend who had started all of this, who had been the first to appear, who had always believed in magic. He smiled, a big, warm, trusting smile at

Jackson. And as he did so, he threw his arms up in the air, as if throwing golden confetti over the crowd and mouthed, "Alacadabrazam!" just as he had done on the first night they had met. Jackson smiled back at him, a big, warm, trusting smile just as the Merry Theatre's curtain opened and he stepped into the light.

THE END

About the Author

Kirstie Rowson is a writer and illustrator. She has published two picture books *Angel's Great Escape: A Christmas Story* and *An Amazing Alphabet of Cake.* This is the first of her Merry Theatre books. Sign up for the newsletter on Kirstie's website to hear more about her books and creative projects.

🌐 www.ifindoubtcreate.co.uk

Printed in Great Britain
by Amazon

52253207R00128